THIS RAGING LIGHT

ESTELLE LAURE

HOUGHTON MIFFLIN HARCOURT ⚡ BOSTON   NEW YORK

All rights reserved. For information about permission to reproduce selections from this book, write to trade.permissions@hmhco.com or to Permissions, Houghton Mifflin Harcourt Publishing Company, 3 Park Avenue, 19th Floor, New York, New York 10016.

www.hmhco.com

The text was set in Norlik and Arquitecta.

Library of Congress Cataloging-in-Publication data is available.

ISBN: 978-0-544-53429-2 hardcover
ISBN: 978-0-544-81321-2 paperback

Manufactured in the United States of America
DOC 10 9 8 7 6 5 4 3 2 1
4500641785

For my children, Lilu Sophia and
Bodhi Lux, who love huge

Day 14

Mom was supposed to come home yesterday after her two-week vacation. Fourteen days. Said she needed a break from everything (*See also:* Us) and that she would be back before the first day of school. I kind of knew she wasn't going to show up, on account of what I got in the mail yesterday, but I waited up all night just the same, hoping, hoping I was just being paranoid, that my pretty-much-never-wrong gut had made some kind of horrible mistake. The door didn't squeak, the floorboards never creaked, and I watched the sun rise against the wall, my all-the-way-insides knowing the truth: we are alone, Wrenny and me, at least for now. Wren and Lucille. Lucille and Wren. I will do whatever

I have to. No one will ever pull us apart. That means keeping things as normal as possible. Faking it. Because things couldn't be further from.

Normal got gone with Dad.

It gave me kind of a funny floating feeling as I brushed Wren's hair into braids she said were way too tight, made coffee, breakfast, lunch for the two of us, got her clothes, her bag, walked her to her first day of fourth grade, saying hi to everyone in the neighborhood while I tried to dodge anyone who might have the stones to ask me where the hell my mother was. But I did it all wrong, see. Out of order.

I should make coffee and get myself ready first. Wren should get dressed after breakfast and not before, because she is such a sloppy eater. As of this morning, she apparently doesn't like tuna ("It looks like puke—ick"), which was her favorite yesterday, and I only found out when it was already packed and we were supposed to be walking out the door. I did the piles of deflated laundry, folded mine, hung up Mom's, carefully placed Wren's into her dresser drawers, but it turns out none of her clothes fit right anymore. How did she grow like that in two measly weeks? Maybe because these fourteen days have been foreverlong.

These are all things Mom did while nobody noticed. I

notice her now. I notice her *isn't*. I notice her *doesn't*. I want to poke at Wren, find out why she doesn't ask where Mom is on the first day of school, why Mom isn't here. Does she know somewhere inside that this was always going to happen, that the night the police came was the beginning and that this is only the necessary, inevitable conclusion?

Sometimes you just know a thing.

Anyway, I did everything Mom would do. At least, I tried to. But the universe knows good and well that I am playing at something, pretending from a manual I wish I had. Still, when I kissed the top of Wren's dark, smooth head goodbye, she skipped into the school building. That's got to count for something.

It's a balmy morning. Summer doesn't know it's on the outs yet, and I quickstep the nine blocks between the schools. By the time I push through the high school doors, I am sweating all over the place.

And now I'm here. In class. The song Wren was humming on the way to school pounds a dull and boring headache through me, some poppy beat. I'm a little late to English, but so is mostly everyone else on the first day. Soon we'll all know exactly where we're supposed to be and when, where we sit. We'll be good little sheople.

Eden is here, always on time, early enough to stake her claim to exactly the seat she wants, her arm draped over the back of an empty chair next to her, until she sees me and drops it to her side. English is the only class we got together this year, which is a ball of suck. First time ever. I like it better when we get to travel through the day side by side. At least our lockers are next to each other's.

She's so cool, but in her totally Eden way. It's not the kind of cool that says come and get me. It's the kind that watches and waits and sees a lot—a thinking kind. Her thick, flaming hair virtually flows over the back of her chair, and her leather-jacket armor is on, which you would think is a little excessive for September in Cherryville, New Jersey, except for the fact that they blast the air conditioning at this school so it's movie-theater cold, and really I'm wishing I had a jacket, wishing I had packed Wren something cozy in her backpack too, but I'm pretty sure it's not quite so bad at the elementary school. I think the high school administration has decided that freezing us out might help control our unruly hormones or something.

They are wrong.

Mr. Liebowitz gives me a look as I sit down. I have so rudely interrupted his standard cranky speech about the year, about how he'll take no guff from us this time around, about how just because we're seniors doesn't mean we get to act like jackasses and get a free pass. Or maybe he's giving me that look because he knows about Dad, too. People titter all around me, but it's like Eden and her leather jacket muffle all that noise right out. As long as I have her, I'm okay. I never mess around much with other people anyway. Digby may be her twin, but I'm the one she shares a brain with.

Meanwhile, Liebowitz looks like Mister Rogers, so he can growl and pace as much as he wants and it has no effect. You know he's a total softie, that he can't wait to get home and change into his cardigan and comfy shoes, so he can get busy taking superspectacular care of his plants and play them Frank Sinatra or something. He'll calm down. He always starts the year uptight. Who can blame him? High school is a total insane asylum. They need bars on the windows, security guards outside. They would never do that here.

Eden kicks her foot into mine and knocks me back into now. I do not like now, and so I kick back, wondering if playing footsies with my best friend qualifies as guff.

"Dinner," she mouths.

"Wren," I mouth back. Shrug.

My eyes tell her about Mom without meaning to.

She shakes her head. Then, "Bitch," she says in a whisper.

I shrug again, try to keep my eyes from hers.

"Bring Wren. My mom will feed the world."

I nod.

"Digby will be there." She kicks my foot again.

I make my whole self very still. Stare at Liebowitz as his thin, whitish lips form words.

"Well, he does live at your house," I say. Superlame.

"Ladies," Liebowitz says, all sing-songy warning. "It's only the first day. Don't make me separate you."

Good luck separating us, I want to say. *Good luck with that. Go feed your fish and water your plants. Get your cardigan and your little sneakers on, and leave me alone.*

It's a beautiful day in the neighborhood. Won't you be my neighbor?

When Wrenny and I roll up the hill to Eden's house in Mom's ancient Corolla, Digby and his dad, John, are outside playing basketball, and I want to get in the house as fast as possible, because otherwise I might be trapped here all day, staring. I get a little twinge of something seeing a dad and his kid playing ball like dads and kids are supposed to. That's a real thing, and my hand wants to cover Wren's face so she can't see all that she is missing.

Which reminds me. "Wren."

"Yeah?" She's wiping at her shirt, reading a book on her lap, and she's a little bit filthy, her hair greasy and knotty in spite of my efforts this morning. At some point the braids came out, and she's reverted to wild.

"You know how Mom hasn't been around lately?"

She stops. Tightens. "Yeah," she says.

"Well, we don't want anyone to know about that, okay? Even Janie and Eden and Digby and John."

"But Mom's on vacation. She's getting her head together. She's coming back."

"Okay, yes," I say, "but still. We don't want to tell anyone, because they might not understand that. They might get the wrong idea."

"Like that she left us permanently?" There is so much more going on inside that Wrenny-head than I can ever know.

"Maybe, or at least for longer than she was supposed to." I reach for the handle to the door because I can't look at her. "Someone might think that."

"She didn't, though," she says. "She's Mom."

"Of course she didn't." Lie.

"So who cares what anyone thinks?"

"Wren, just don't, okay?"

"Okay."

"Some things are private." I open the door, then lean back across and wipe uselessly at her shirt with my thumb. "Like Mom being on vacation. So, okay?"

"I said okay, okay?" She gets out and waits, stares at me like I'm the most aggravating person on earth. "Hey, Lu?"

"Yeah?" I say, bracing myself for what's next.

"Your mama's so fat, she left the house in high heels and came back in flip-flops."

I would tell her that I hate her new obsession with "your mama" jokes, but I'm not in the mood for any dawdling, so I half laugh and get moving. I want to get inside and quick because there's also the other thing. And by "other" I mean what makes me sweat just standing here. And by "thing" I mean Digby, who I have known since I was seven but who lately makes a fumbling moronic moron out of me, a full-on half-wit. Ask me my name when I'm in his presence and I'm not likely to be able to tell you. I'd probably just say "Lllll . . .

llllllllu . . ." and you'd have to catch the drool running down my chin.

I know. It's not at all attractive.

But really. Tall, sweaty, and *not* wearing a shirt, so the muscles are all right there for the watching. He doesn't exactly glisten, on account of the fact that he's whiter than white, that he tans by getting freckles, so he's covered in them now after a whole summer outside. But seeing his hair all plastered to his forehead, his body so long and lean, looping around his dad to get the ball into the hoop, I want to fall out of the car and onto my knees in the driveway, say *Lord have mercy, hallelujah*, write sonnets and paint him, and worship that one little curve where his neck meets his shoulder that is just so, so perfect.

He is beautiful.

Which is why when he says hi as I pass him, I barely raise a pinky in response. There are two main problems here, aside from the fact that he is Eden's twin and that's all kinds of weird. One, he's had the same girlfriend since the dawn of time. They're pinned, she wears his jacket, their marriage certificate is practically already signed. Angels bless their freakin' union. And two, if I ever did get a chance with him, like if he ever kissed me or something, I would die of implosion. I know I sound like a twelve-year-old mooning over some celebrity, and not the extremely self-possessed woman-to-be that I actually am, but something about him makes me lose my mind. Something about the way he moves, about his himness — it shatters me all the way down. So I hope he never does kiss me. That would be nothing but a disaster. No one needs to see me fall apart like that. Least of all him.

Actually, maybe least of all me.

Eden's mom, Janie, made meatballs. She doesn't know how to cook for just four people or even six, since she's a caterer and party planner, so the fridge is always full of these hors d'oeuvres-ish leftovers. If she's going to make a dish, she makes a lot of it. You can tell from the smell in the house that the meatballs have been simmering in sauce all day. Meatball essence has found its way into everything.

I watch them for a minute, Eden and Janie. Two red-heads, working together over the counter in the big, brand-new open kitchen, backs to us. Everything is just-so here in their dream house, exactly the way they wanted it, so the kitchen somehow looks like an extension of Janie. Eden and her mom look so much alike, except Janie has a more put-together thing than Eden, who is in her ballet getup as she always is outside of school, as though she's returning to a necessary skin. Janie bumps her butt into Eden's. Eden bumps back. Butt footsies. Eden is into footsies of all types. They are chopping vegetables for the salad, both stringy and efficient, and together. I put my arm around Wren and pull her into my waist just as Beaver Cleaver, the goldendoodle, jumps on her, and Janie sees us.

"Hi, girls," she says.

"Hi, Janie," Wren says, immediately collapsing onto the floor with BC.

I wave.

"It smells really good in here," Wren says from under white fur. "Are you making vodka sauce?"

Janie smiles. "Vodka sauce? That's a little advanced, isn't it?"

"Food Network," Wren says, jumping to her feet, "and also Gino's. They have good vodka sauce over there."

"Well"—Janie points to the cabinet in the dining room,

and I start pulling out dishes—"that's very impressive, Wren. No, this is not a vodka sauce. It's plain old marinara, but hopefully you'll like it."

"Oh yeah," Wren says. "I will like it. We've been eating frozen pizza for weeks."

"Have not," I say. That really is a gross exaggeration.

"Yeah, everything Lucille makes is from a box."

We had a lot of pizza in the freezer.

"What about your mom?" Janie says. "She's not bad in the kitchen."

"She's not here," Wren says, then looks at me with a what-am-I-supposed-to-say shrug. "'Cause she's on vacation," she adds.

"Oh, right," Janie says. Her face pinches.

"Maybe you want to watch some TV until dinner?" Eden says, wedging between Janie and Wren.

"Ten minutes," Janie says, turning back to the kitchen a bit reluctantly. "Finish setting the table, girls." It feels good to take orders.

"You know," Eden says, "there is something really messed up and sexist about the fact that we are all in here cooking and acting like domesticated livestock while the males are outside playing basketball."

"Oh, for god's sake, Eden," Janie says as she pours dressing into the big wooden salad bowl. "I love to cook."

"His Royal Highness could at least set the table." Glasses clink.

"I thought he could use a little time with your dad."

"Yes, he could. Setting the table. Doing something besides displaying his Neanderthal abilities. You're encouraging and perpetuating male privilege, you know."

"Eden, I'm making dinner for my family, which is a joy for me." She emits a giant sigh. "I shouldn't have to defend it. And it's no crime to let them play every once in a while."

"Yeah, but when do *we* get to play, Mom? That's my question."

My eyes fill. My breath gets weird. They're so stupid, arguing over this. They don't know. They don't know.

"Lucille," Janie says over Eden's head, "would you do me a favor and grab the boys? Tell them dinner is about ready."

Drat.

How does a person go from being like a decorative component in the house that is your life — a nice table, perhaps — to being the pipes, the foundation, the center beam, without which the entire structure falls apart? How does a barely noticeable star become your very own sun?

How is it that one day Digby was Eden's admittedly extra-cute brother, and then the next he stole air, gave jitters, twisted my insides all up? Is this hormones? A glitch in the matrix? A product of internal desperation and my lack of developed self?

I have tried a million times to puzzle out the moment he turned so vital, and I can't do it. I only know that my stupid, annoying feelings have completely compromised my ability to function around him, that I want to close the space between us and wrap myself around him. My whole being would exhale, I think. It's ridiculous.

Which is why I stare at my plate. So hard I stare at my plate. I eat my meatball (I can only seem to stomach one), while Eden and Digby throw one-liners at each other. Nobody notices much, and I am afraid to look up, because Digby is exactly across the table from me.

Wren stuffs meatballs all in her face. Sauce drips down the front of her shirt.

"Oh my gosh," she says to Janie, "you're, like, a culinary genius."

Janie beams in my peripheral vision.

"You come here anytime you want," she says. "You are officially my favorite guest." She spears some asparagus, smiles, and says, "Culinary." Shakes her head. "So, Lucille, how long is your mother out of town for?"

Forever. "She should be back in the next couple of days."

"Is she doing okay?" *Since,* she wants to say. *After.* Janie looks so intense all the time.

Wren tilts her head toward me, and I unfreeze.

"You're doing all right by yourselves down there?" Janie presses.

"Oh, totally," I say, going in for some asparagus myself. "Mom will be back."

It all stops. The movement at the table.

"Of course," Janie says. Her fork *tic-tic-tics* against the plate. "Obviously she's coming back." She takes a bite and chews. "I've left a couple of messages for her, you know. Just checking to see if she needs some help. She hasn't returned my calls." Straight to voice mail. Yeah, I know all about it. "She must really be enjoying her time away. She must need it." There's something in her tone that doesn't register on her face.

I make myself meet her eyes. Nod. Present a meek smile. On the way back to my plate, those traitorous jellies that live in my head rest on Digby's, and roller-coaster rush number 892 thrashes through me. He drops his eyes, twists spaghetti, and pays really close attention to his mom and what she is now saying about the wedding she is catering this weekend.

I thud, kick Eden under the table. Mean footsies.

He knows about my mother.

Digby knows.

"All things truly wicked begin from an innocence," Eden says.

Janie has Wren making some kind of cookie thing, so we are in Eden's room after dinner, and she is stretching and bending in a way that makes me uncomfortable because those are things the human body shouldn't do. Also, her feet are disgusting, and I have to look away when she pokes one of them in my face, not on purpose but because she is in the midst of some bananas contortionist move.

"Sick," I say to a bunion, to a ripped purple nail, to a bloody flap of skin.

"Hemingway," she says, and flutter, flutter, flutter goes the foot.

"Seriously, you need to do something about that. It looks infected."

"Baloney," she says. "Are you listening to me?"

"Hemingway," I say, wondering how this will ever help me in my life.

"Nobody *means* to be a douchebag, much less wicked."

"Serial killers?"

"Even them, I bet. Personality disorders complicate my theory, but you have to figure even they were cute little babies once upon a time. They can't help it that they got the raw end of the human gene stick. Compassion," she says.

"You called her a bitch."

"That's what I'm saying."

"That my mother is wicked?" Sometimes I wish she would just spit it out instead of making me work so hard.

"No. That she's not. That her behavior is. That it stems from innocence . . ."

"But she's still a douchebag."

"And a bitch."

"Nice," I say, like it's not nice, which it's not.

"But I still have compassion for her. It can't be easy. But now for you," she says.

"For me." Numbers start dancing in my head.

I stare at the ceiling, the spot over where Eden sleeps. BEWARE, GENTLE KNIGHT reads the piece of paper taped across the ceiling. THERE IS NO GREATER MONSTER THAN REASON.

"Believe it," she says, pointing up with a particularly nasty toe.

"I have to pee," I say.

"McCarthy," she says as I make my escape.

Into Digby, who is going down the hall in the opposite direction, wet, with a clean T-shirt and shorts on, which feels weirdly intimate. He was recently in the nude.

He reaches for me. His hand moves from his side, where it was just dangling, not doing much of anything. Now it is awake and touching. It traces my shoulder, skips down my arm, slides across my hand. And then he's gone. He keeps walking. He never even looked at me.

I fall into a family portrait. I'm surprised that the earthquake inside me doesn't bring the entire wall of pictures tumbling down. My skin burns. All the blood in my body charges for the spots he touched.

A war.

A fight to the death.

Sometimes, I think as I wander into the steamy bathroom like a half-starved zombie, something slow happens fast and you can't quite grasp the moment, whether it was an important one, whether it actually happened or you made it up. It's already like that. Did he really do that? Did he really run his hand across me like that? Did he? Was he taking liberties? And oh snap, double snap, if this is what happens to me from one tiny finger, then take what I said before about the should-not-ever-kiss thing and times it by about a jillion.

There is a scar now on my arm, where he touched me. It forms on my skin, watery blue, shimmery sort of, like how burns get shiny sometimes, after. How the burnt skin is new at the same time as it's forever damaged.

I am dramatic.

Flush. Wash. Wander.

Eden.

"What the hell is wrong with you?" she says, petting BC, who has flopped himself onto her bed and is lying across her lap, panting.

I give her a look.

"Are you high? Did you fall into a K-hole while you were gone?"

What if Digby can hear her from wherever he is?

"Cookies!" Wren calls from the kitchen. She sounds delighted.

When we have reconvened around the table and are scarfing down chocolate-chip-oatmeal cookies (except Eden, who would never), Digby slips by. He still doesn't look at me. There is no secret connection. He grabs the ball by the door, nods in the general direction of the table, and is gone.

It's four o'clock in the morning. My belly is digesting a single meatball, too much bubbly water, and several cookies. Obviously, I am having trouble sleeping.

In my right hand I hold a pile of paper. Within these many folds of paper are numbers. Bills. Electric. Oil. Car insurance. Now quarterly bills that piled in last week. Water. Sanitation. And then there's the phone. That, too. That one must be paid. If Mom ever does decide to call, it has to be working. We need food, and Wrenny needs new clothes, and me too for that matter, although let's just call that one a for-get-about-it-for-eternity.

My right hand shakes harder.

In my left—yes, my left hand, ladies and gentlemen, boys and girls—I hold a crisp and shiny one-hundred-dollar bill. That is how I know she is still alive. That is what I got in the mail yesterday. That is how I know that somewhere my mother is still walking this earth. She didn't get hit in the head. She doesn't have amnesia. She isn't dead in a gutter somewhere. She is simply not here. She is somewhere else. One hundred dollars that came in an envelope with no return address, and a postmark so I know it came from California. She must be there with long-lost friends, maybe rediscovering her past or something. A note: *I'm trying. Love you, Mom.* That's it. That's all she wrote, folks.

What does it mean? She's trying to get back to us? Trying to get better? Trying to get a job? Maybe it's just her way of keeping us from sending the FBI out to look for her. Effective tactic. I wish my last memories of her were of some-one I recognized, someone whose behavior I could predict. It kind of makes me want to tower over her with my hands on my hips and tell her that trying is just not good enough, young lady.

Yeah, Mom. I'm trying too.

I trail the hundred across my field of vision, let it tickle at my eyelashes. There was a time when a one-hundred-dollar bill would have been the most exciting thing, the promise of a free-for-all at the toy store, something to be tucked away for an indulgent moment.

Not now. Now it's part of a great big equation that adds up to me being totally screwed. I know she meant to come back. She didn't leave me the bank card or checks or anything that I've been able to find. She would have left me something if she thought she was going forever. She is not wicked, or at least she didn't start out that way. Still, she isn't here, and I don't have what I need to do this job. All she left me was her car and this house.

And Wren.

My left hand is a fist.

Day 27

I'm in the park. It's a beautiful day. The sun is shining, birds are chirping, a cool breeze is blowing. The kind of day I always wish for here, a rare one that's not too humid or too cold. Just perfect. Too bad I'm fluttering on the inside, having trouble breathing.

We're almost out of food. I have officially scoured the house for every last bit of change. In jars, under couch pillows, deep in pockets. I took a bag of dusty quarters, crusty dimes, and sticky nickels to the machine at the Super Fresh and traded it all in for dollars, and not many at that. How many more days before I am on my knees in front of some social worker, begging her to leave me my sister, to leave me that at least?

Wren is on the swings, going high, laughing with a friend. She has been playing with this girl, Melanie, at school and I want her to feel normal, so I'm here even though I have so much to do. Melanie has braids with little beads on the ends and is decked out from head to toe in shiny things. I like watching them there, swinging easily on such a nice day, even though every time the swing goes up I think *bills* and every time it goes down I think *money*. Melanie's sister, Shane, is next to me on the bench. They're kind of new around here, and the high school is where they put the whole county, so it's easy enough not to know everyone, but now I have to know her. At least a little.

She's been asking me questions in between texts. She gets a lot of them, so she's pretty busy, and she does a lot of laughing, says oh-no-you-did-not when she reads them. Yesterday she started talking to me. I want to ask her questions, but I don't want to answer any, so I stay quiet, keep my hands on my lap.

"Ten minutes!" Shane yells at Melanie. "And I don't want to have to tell you twice." Her phone vibrates. She checks it. Shakes her head. "Guys are stupid, don't you think? Always coming when you don't want them, running when you do."

I smile. Nod. Of course they come to her. She's all dark and exotic and self-confident but accessible. She looks like fun.

"You got a boyfriend?" she asks.

"No."

"You gay?"

"No!"

"Homophobic?"

"Oh my gosh!"

She makes fun. Giggles.

"Working?" she asks.

"Me?"

"No. Your parents. That's your sister, right?"

"Yes."

"So your mom is working?"

"No." Why did I say that?

"Where is she, then?"

I shrug. My throat gets bigger than it has room for.

"You on your own?"

She says it like it's the simplest thing, and her questions are so rapid-fire that I don't have time to think.

"With her?" she asks.

I don't say anything. Even though I know that no response is a response, I won't say it out loud. I don't know this girl, but something deep inside says *trust her*. My quiet doesn't seem to matter to Shane, who looks at me sharpish. It's useless. I can already tell she's the kind of person who sees things as they are. Something in the angle of her head.

"I had this friend, Janine, back home, I mean in Hoboken. She took care of her two baby brothers forever. They had this whole thing going with welfare, though. Her mom was on it, so when she split, Janine got the checks. It worked for a while. Hard on her, though." She pauses. "You on welfare?"

I might projectile.

"I'm hungry, Lu," Wren calls to me. "Can we go to Eden's?"

No, we can't go to Eden's.

"My mom's a nurse in Flemington," Shane goes on like she didn't hear. "That's how we got here to the damn boonies. She only works three days a week, but crazy hours. Mostly weekends." Points to Melanie. "So I have that little piece of work to deal with those days, then my own job the rest. Not bad, though. She's all right." She takes a stick of gum from her purse. Offers me one. I actually accept it, and it's yummy. "All right for a hot mess." She leans into me with her shoulder. Nudges me in a way that would usually make me want to push back. I don't, though.

"So you take care of her?" I try. "When your mom is at work?"

Shane smiles like she won something. I know it's because I finally said a complete sentence. She leans in.

"Yeah, it's a pain in the ass some days, but you do what you gotta do."

"What you gotta do," I say, thinking of all the things I gotta do.

"You're all kinds of locked up, you know that?" Shane says. She looks at me. "You need to loosen up." She peers at me, gives me a good once-over. "You got enough money?"

I immediately almost cry.

"You could get a job," she says. "You know Fred's? He's looking for a busser, like, now."

Yes. I know Fred's. Everybody does. Reviewed in every major magazine, so people come from all over. Fred is supposed to be some kind of crazy food god with a posse of busty babes at his side. I've never been in there. Part performance art, part Mexican restaurant, all wild. Or so legend has it. Scary.

"Oh," she says, wrinkling her nose. "I see. You're too good for that place."

That's not what I meant.

She signals Melanie from across the park, and Melanie completely ignores her. "Too bad," she says, lifting her sunglasses to check her phone again. "I made two hundred last night."

Two hundred pays electric. In one night?

Wren skips over, takes my hand. "Let's gooooo . . ." she whines. "I'm hungry."

"Feed that? Need a job," Shane says, standing. "Get your butt off that swing, Mel. We gotta go!" Blows a bubble and snaps it at me. "When you get off your high horse, come into the restaurant. I think he'll hire you if you come in quick. We just lost someone. Threw her apron on the floor and walked out. Couldn't take the heat."

"I'm not . . ."

"I know about your dad," she whispers so Wren can't hear. "He's crazy, right?"

I know my face changes color.

Wren lets go of me, runs to meet Melanie.

"It's all right." Shane taps my shoulder. "Everyone's crazy, girl. You learn that after a while. Just depends which kind and whether you want it or not. That's what you decide. The rest is out of your hands."

"Look what Melanie taught me," Wrenny says, and she and Melanie do some kind of jumping-slapping-their-own-behinds thing that is surprisingly complex and rhythmic for a couple of nine-year-olds.

"Awesome!" I say, trying not to show that my pulse got all wonky when Shane mentioned Dad.

We clap, and I grab Wrenny's backpack from next to the bench. Rub my hand along the silent, soon-to-be-turned-off cell phone in my pocket and my very last ten-dollar bill.

"Fred's?" I say. "You really think he'd hire me?"

"Atta girl," Shane says back. "You got a phone number?"

Trust. What does it even mean? You hand somebody the knife to stab you with when you trust them. I know this much is true. I jitter and skitter, but Shane can help me put food in my fridge, keep my lights on, keep the cable for Wren's cooking shows, keep us together.

My hand may have been shaking, but I had to give that
stranger-girl the knife, even knowing how sharp it might be.

Digby holds one knife.

Eden another.

And now Shane.

That's a lot of knives.

I feel the prickle-tickle of the blades at my throat and
hope the hands holding them are steady.

So . . .

With my last ten dollars I buy:

> half a pound of ham
> one loaf of white bread (the only kind I can get
>   Wren to eat)
> two Cokes (don't you judge me)
> iceberg lettuce (I know: no nutritional value)
> one apple (Fuji — the only kind I like, never mealy)

We eat our sandwiches outside, because it's just too nice to be
cooped up. We gulp down our sodas, and while Wren talks

and sings, I remember when Eden and Digby lived next door, how our porch was communal since our houses were connected. When we were smaller, Eden and I would leave stuff for each other on the white railing that divided our porch in half. If Eden forgot her shoes at my house, I would just stick them there and they'd be gone the next time I looked. Back when I had time to read, Eden would leave books on the railing for me with little sticky notes on pages she liked. Eden and Digby lived on the pretty, functional side, while I was stuck in the warped, funhouse world. Because let's face it, we used to be a family when Mom and Dad were around, but we were never *them*. I never thought any of it would change. I didn't understand yet that everything always changes. It's a law of the universe. I wish someone had told me that. I wasn't paying close enough attention to the fact that they were there. They were a permanent fixture. I thought they'd stay forever.

But they moved on while we slipped backwards.

Then came Mrs. Albertson with her curlers and her bottomless glass of lemonade, which is what she is holding now as she eases onto the rocker where Eden's lounge chair used to rest against the house's brick face. She nods her head at us. "Hi, girls."

We wave but keep eating. We are hungry.

"How's everyone?"

"We're good." Wrenny shoves the last of her sandwich into her mouth. "Want to see what I learned at the park?"

She launches into her dance moves. Right now they look more perverted than amazingly impressive. Must there be so much gyration?

"Mmmm," Mrs. Albertson says, her judgment wedged between her wrinkles.

I need to sweep the porch.

"How's your mother?" she asks.

"Fine," I say. The sandwich gets too big for my mouth, won't go down when I try to swallow. "Busy."

Wren leans against the back of the porch, goes utterly still.

"Haven't seen her lately."

"No, she's working a lot. Got a job nursing in Flemington. Crazy hours." It just came out.

"Oh." Mrs. Albertson takes a sip of her lemonade, looking confused. "I didn't know she was a nurse."

"Yeah," I say. "Before she had Wren. She's been working really hard to get her degree up-to-date in New Jersey and everything, and now she did it. I'm really proud of her. She's working so much. She's so tired from working so hard for us." Overkill. *Take it down a notch.* I don't ever talk this much. It will look suspicious.

Wren taps her finger along the rail. Hums loudly.

"Well, tell her I said hello," Mrs. Albertson says.

"Will do," I say. I never say that. "And how are you?" My heart is beating speedy quick, and I just want to go inside, but I don't want to look like I'm running.

"Oh, I'm fine. Still wondering why on earth I bought this house. When Geoffrey passed and all five kids were gone, it seemed logical to downsize a bit. But my legs are only going to get worse, you know?" She rubs at her thigh. "I should have considered the stairs." She takes another sip from her glass. "I suppose I ought to be grateful that I can still have sugar. No diabetes yet." She knocks on the railing and smiles.

"I guess we all have to be grateful for the little things." It seems like the right thing to say.

Mrs. Albertson leans so far forward that I can see the wrinkly, wobbly cleavage she hides in her button-down shirts. "Yes, Miss Lucille," she says. "I do believe that's all there is."

⚡

I shuffle Wrenny past the flapping screen door, through the scratched-up wooden one, and into the peace of our broke-down palace. Well, peace, I guess that's debatable. More hushed than peaceful. A weird silence takes over. Wren is almost never this quiet.

As we pass through the house I see:

> The tile needs replacing, and the toilet seat has come loose in the bathroom.

> The doorknob on the back bedroom has come off, so you need a screwdriver to get it open whenever it accidentally shuts all the way.

> Something is wrong with the water heater too. Hot water only comes when the dishwasher is on, which can't be right.

> The other night, the towel rack just came off the wall when I was trying to put the towel up after Wren's bath. I need to put it back.

This house has been possessed by some pissed-off spirit that knows my parents are gone and has decided to rip everything apart.

We crawl into Mom's bed, and I flip on the good ole

Food Network. Blessed be, Wrenny's favorite show is on. The Barefoot Contessa smiles beatifically at us. She roasts her roast as Wren relaxes into me.

Mom was going to paint the sky in Wrenny's room. That's how she put it. A week before she left she got a hundred sample squares and let Wrenny pick out the color. Mom actually got the paint and everything. I thought she was better, and then she tried to see Dad that last time, and when she found out he had been released and left instructions for his information to stay confidential, even from his wife, it all went to hell. She completely lost it. But for a day or two before that she seemed really excited. Motivated to put the pieces back together or something. I thought we had her again.

Wren chose I've Got the Blues as her color. Said she wanted the sky in her room since she only has a little window in there, and Mom said if it was sky she wanted, then sky she should have.

The unopened cans are still sitting under the foot stains from Wrenny lying with dirty heels against the wall. I guess it's moot, though, that it never happened. My sister hasn't spent a night in her own room since Mom left. Neither of us has. We've been in Mom's room instead, since it has a bed that fits the both of us and the TV is in there. I think at first we were keeping the bed warm for her, but now it's warm for us. Together. The door to Wren's room is mostly closed, except for when she goes in to get something or put something in. We like it that way.

Shadows fall. Wren holds on tight.

When Mom would put her to bed, she'd sing her a song or read her a book until she fell asleep. Some nights when I got into bed early, their pillow talk was like a fan humming laughter and music to carry me to my dreams. Me? I stare at the ceiling, one hand on Wren's back. Air in. Air out. Life.

Mom left with a single suitcase and a computer bag, said she was going to gather her thoughts and she would be back soon. She said we could reach her by phone and that she would call every day either way. When we asked where she was going, she said she didn't know. She must have known something though. She was going somewhere. Gave us a freezer full of food and a few hundred dollars, told me all the bills were paid for the month, and then walked out. She was a little slurry, kind of wide-eyed and dull. She barely hugged us when she got into the cab to the airport.

It was like we weren't there, like we were ghosts. But by

then she was a shell. The Mom I knew was already gone, had been for a while. So saying goodbye wasn't so much saying goodbye as it was letting go of the last of something that was a fading memory anyway.

She never called.

Now Wren holds me around the waist, almost unconscious. She rests her head on my shoulder. Her hair smells like wet dog, not because she actually came into contact with a wet dog but because (I have discovered) little girls smell like wet dog when they don't wash their hair and their tween hormones come out of their skulls. She drapes her arm over my stomach, hits the mute button on the remote.

"Mom's not a nurse," she says, muffled into me.

"No," I say.

"You said she is."

"I did, Wrenny girl."

"Okay," she says.

I want to ask the top of Wren's head what we're going to do. What does the future look like now? All I see is a black hole, an empty space where college and boys and food should be. If I don't do something, pretty soon the house will disintegrate and fall into the ground. Someone will find out we're here alone, Wren and I will have to leave and we will be separated, and my cell phone will be disconnected. Mom won't be able to get in touch if something happens to her. And if she does come back, she will have that slack look on her face. She won't try hard enough to get better. She won't fight. And we will all be lost and listing in oblivion.

Hundred-dollar bills from wandering souls aren't going to cut it.

Wren is snoring. I have been staring at the ceiling for a ka-jillion years.

My phone vibrates under my pillow. I don't even briefly think it's Mom. Only one person ever texts me at this time of night.

KNOCK KNOCK, it says. Eden.

WHO'S THERE? I manage to type, over Wrenny's head.

GET THEE TO THE RIVER

GIVE ME 30

We have a spot. You go a little way up the tow path and then cross over, past the old train car. We don't know how the train car wound up nestled between trees, wedged among rocks. We've always wondered why no one goes there but us, since it's so obviously the coolest spot in town. It's the perfect place to stare at the river and talk about stuff. We used to spend hours dipping our toes into the water on hot days, surrounded by lush green and sweet shade, back when we decided to be BFFs and had fake-gold necklaces to prove it. We even took a botched blood oath. Eden was in charge. The cuts took weeks to heal. Kind of like when she pierced my ears right on her rock. I should not allow her to wield sharp objects near my person.

So much has happened at this spot.

Now we meet at night, in the dark, because it's the only time we have to really be alone. And before you judge me about leaving Wrenny home, consider that she once slept through an earthquake at Disneyland and that we live in probably the safest place on earth. Anyway, whatever. Call me irresponsible.

I swear Eden is a lighthouse. Perched on her favorite rock in her leg warmers and black hoodie, she looks like she's glowing in the dark, which hardly makes sense considering what she's wearing. I think it's her freakishly pale skin.

I hug her for longer than I should. It's different here than at school, or even her house. It's just the two of us, no witnesses. I like to think that the things we talk about here are safe, that words drip from our mouths into the earth and grow trees that guard secrets in their leaves.

"I'm scared," I say before I am even all the way sitting.

"I know." She holds on to her knees and angles her head to the side, a lithe, bright tree fairy.

"Mrs. Albertson is asking questions and the house is falling apart, and Wrenny, I don't know what's going on with her and I can't see the future anymore when I look for it in my head."

She slips hair behind her ear.

"At least you don't have rent or a mortgage. Praise be to your Aunt Jan." She crosses herself. "May god rest her soul, of course."

"Taxes," I offer. "The bill came today."

"You need some help, Lu," she says. "You're not going to be able to do this alone." She pulls a smoke out of her pocket. All ballerinas smoke, she says. Weight. I like the smell of it, how it almost reaches my lungs too. Somehow it isn't horrible on her the way it is on others. Maybe that's because the rest of her smells like honeysuckle and rock salt. It all comes together pleasing, like a really complicated piece of chocolate. She takes a long drag. Ashes. "Well, I guess you only have nine months until you turn eighteen, right?"

I know she means to comfort me, but that sounds like forever to hold it all together. And it's the first time anyone's said that Mom might really not come back. And what happens when I turn eighteen? At the stroke of midnight on my birthday everything magically gets fixed? Maybe I could get guardianship of Wren, but what happens after? What about the rest of my life?

"Don't let my mom find out," she says. "She will do exactly the wrong thing. And she's been asking questions. She's not stupid." She pulls something from her pocket. Shoves bills into my hand. A no-nonsense tree fairy. "I think you should stay away from my house for a while. Lie low. Maybe she'll forget to involve herself. Meanwhile, buy groceries. And let me think. We'll figure this out."

"'We,'" I say, staring at the money in my palm. It's enough for lunch supplies for the next couple of days. Money I would like to give back but can't. Guilt. Shame. Joy. So many things.

"Of course 'we.'" She smiles. "You're my BFFFFFFF."

I giggle. She made me giggle. It feels like so long since I've done that. Eons.

I slip the money into my pocket, take her in again.

"Do you think my mom loves us?" I ask.

She watches me for too long, chooses her words so carefully. "It doesn't matter if she loves you or not." She tucks long fingers inside her sleeves, lets them dangle.

"Really?" I say.

"'All feeling has an equivalent in action or is useless.'"

"Did you say that?"

"Of course not," she says. "Virginia Woolf."

"Oh."

"You know what I think, my li'l Lulu?" Eden pulls her zipper up and down like she's hoping the answer will spill out of her chest if she does it enough times. I know how much she wants to have answers for me. "I think that your mom loves you. She might love you so much that she cries all damn day. She might be that sorry." She looks at me, right through me to the other side and back again. "But if she doesn't show up, if she can't — for whatever messed-up reason that allows her to stay away knowing everything you've been through, everything you will have to endure without her—then you just tell me, Miss Lovely Lu, you just tell me what the fuck difference it makes."

In the name of action, Eden and I put on our pragmatic hats. She pulls a pen and her little quote notebook from her pocket and we come up with a list.

> **STEP ONE:** Answer Shane's text and go to that job interview at Fred's tomorrow even though it's really, really scary.

> **STEP TWO:** Eden will watch Wrenny for me two days a week at my house if I get it, so that I can go to said job. She will pretend she's at ballet for extra days. Four hundred dollars a week should do it. Barely, but it will make a big difference.

> **STEP THREE:** Pay the bills one at a time, in order of importance. Strangely, cell phone and cable are at the top. Well, after electric.

> **STEP FOUR:** Go to school and make sure Wrenny goes to school and does homework so that no one gets suspicious.

> **STEP FIVE:** Smile some.

43

Eden writes this, makes a loopy smiley face, rips the page from her notebook, and stuffs the list into my hand.

"That's a start," she says. Looks at me sly.

"What?"

"Nothing."

"No, what?"

"I'm just trying to picture you in short shorts."

"Shut up," I say.

"I don't think overalls are on the menu at Fred's."

"Oh my gosh."

"Or saying 'Oh my gosh.'"

"Oh my gosh!"

"You're going to need a makeover."

"Shut up."

"And to expand your vocabulary," she says. "'Shut up' and 'Oh my gosh' aren't going to cut it. Work on 'Hey there, mister, how do you like your taco? Soft? Or hard?'" She says "hard" so sick. Pushes her chest forward and shakes.

"Ew!" I say, and we are laughing so much. Then I think out loud. "He'll never hire me."

"Oh yes he will," she says. "You have a thing — you just have layers on you." She flits her leg out across my face like she does. "You'll have to take. Them. Off." Gets serious. "Just pretend you're a theater geek and it's a school play or some-thing." This is a preposterous notion. The strength of a thou-sand Mr. Universes could not persuade me to the stage.

"Anyway, you're not eight anymore," she says, glowing mischief into the black. "Buy some lip gloss, for crying out loud."

Day 28

"So what did I say?" Eden grills me.

We are in front of Fred's right at the edge of town, sitting in Mom's car. I am here for my interview, trying to steal a glimpse through the rectangular building's reflective windows to no avail. Eden is biting her thumb, which means she's worried.

"You told me to be brave," I tell her so she knows I remember her instructions.

"Right." Eden acts like this is all I will need if I can just hear it clearly enough. "'Be bold and mighty forces will come to your aid.'" Peers at me. "That's a good one, you know. You should commit it to memory."

"Okay," I say. "But I don't want you to be disappointed if I don't get it."

"Stop. You'll get it. You look great." She picks at my V-neck T-shirt, pulls it down at the front. I pull it back up. "You have to show a little body. Just a little. Mini-cleavage."

"Okay." I pull the shirt back down some.

"You look like Mom," Wrenny says.

"I borrowed from her closet."

"That's not why," Wren says, and I feel funny.

"All right, little girl," Eden says, throwing the car in reverse before I'm even all the way out. "Let's go have some fun."

"Yay!" Wren says.

"And there will be dancing. Oh yes there will."

"Yay!" she says again.

"Text me when you're done and I'll come back for you."

I nod.

They drive away with the music up loud.

Apparently I am not sexy enough.

"What the hell is this?"

Fred looks like a mad scientist, not a restaurant owner.

Salt-and-pepper hair, horn-rimmed glasses, shorts, socks pulled up to his knees, and clogs. I don't know what I was expecting with all the gossip about him and his eccentricities, but not this. This is a whole other thing. He's like Hunter S. Thompson the chef. Gastronomical gonzo. Eden would love him.

Shane, decked out in the required short shorts and black tank, which she is totally pulling off, smacks him on the shoulder.

"Beth quit, right? This is my friend Lucille. Hire her and be quiet. She's here to save your ass."

"Hunh. Is that a Jimi Hendrix thing? Your name?"

I am impressed. No one gets that. I nod.

He points a skinny finger at me. "What is she wearing, Rach? This girl look like one of us to you?"

"Come on, Freddie. She's cute, even in boring clothes." This from perhaps the most gorgeous human I've ever seen. Platinum blond hair, a body that makes my non-gay self want to weep, and eyes so big you could just fall in. "Rachel," she says in the softest voice, and she takes my hand in hers. A limp handshake. "Nice to meet you." Marilyn Monroe liveth.

"Does she talk?" he asks. He wipes clean, wet hands on

his apron, then rests his palms on his waist, Peter Pan–style. He fairly vibrates, and I'm pretty sure he hates me. I knew I wasn't right for this. How did I let Eden talk me into it?

Two hundred dollars, I think. *Stack of bills,* I think.

I try a smile.

"Oh, girl, stop that," Shane whispers in my ear. "That does not look good."

"I talk," I say to Fred, willing myself to meet his eyes.

He smiles a weaselish smile. "Well okay, then, Talkie Talkerton, I got a question for you. Are you ready for war?"

"We love war," Shane says. "Right, girl?"

Generally speaking, I am a pacifist, but I nod, say, "I totally love war."

"Good, because this floor is a battleground, and when I say 'go' we are shooting bullets. My food is grenades you drop. Pull the pin, baby. We are special ops, got it?"

I nod, follow with a "Yes, yes, special ops."

A few girls have wandered in and are doing things behind him. Cutting lemons and limes, filling plastic bottles with honey, rolling silverware. Listening to Fred rant and making faces at each other behind him, but grinning and happy, too. This is a good sign. But Fred seems all kinds of crazy. Which reminds me of what Shane said. How we are all some kind of crazy. I think I might like Fred's particular brand.

"You listening to me?" he says.

"Yes, I'm listening."

"The way I see it"—he paces around in front of me, does a shuffle step—"I open at five and close at ten. You're a member of Freddie's Special Forces from when you get here at four until you're done mopping and shit."

"Okay."

"You don't mess with my food, with my team, we'll be all right. We're family, and I will have your back, see?"

He pauses until I say yes. Then he's at it again.

"Okay, good. I need you four nights a week, Monday through Thursday. You want weekends, you have to earn it or someone from my weekend crew has to die."

Four nights. I told Eden two, and no one is going to believe that ballet goes until after ten. I don't know what else to do, though. I have to take this job, and I have a feeling Fred isn't all that into negotiating.

"So let's do this," he says.

I twitch. I'm hired?

"I'm hired?" I say.

"You'll be Rachel's busser, so you get waters for people, get drinks. Ask Val to grab your alcohol for you, and clean up after people. Get straws and sides of sour cream. Run checks, whatever needs doing. Make sure people are happy and taken care of. Never leave the floor without taking something off a table, and never come back without bringing something with you. You have to move in here. There's no sitting down. We'll see how you do." He gives a crooked smirk. "We'll just see." He turns to Shane, who is filling ketchups in the far corner. "She can't work like this, though. Can you do something about the clothes?"

"Wait . . . I'm working right now?"

"I'll see what's in the back," Shane says, and she throws me the kind of wink that is both cute and confident and also tells me not to argue.

"You have a nice body and a good face." He swivels back to me on his silly clogs. "My special-ops force is a bunch of badass chicks with taco guns. We are burrito snipers, tamale bombers." He throws a few punches in the air. "We are family, but I like my family sexy, so figure out how to work what you got and we'll be okay."

"And how to carry a tray with fourteen waters on it," Rachel says, somehow gliding instead of clomping in her dangerous high heels. "Don't worry, you'll be fine. We all had a first day."

"Okay," I say, thinking about two hundred dollars in my pocket if I can just get through this. "Make me hot so I can be all special ops and stuff."

A girl with black hair, blunt bangs, and red fingernails, covered in tattoos, hoots. Val. "Come on, girl, let's get your paperwork done," she says. "You got this."

Oh my gosh, whispers the fish out of water panicking in my head. *I hope so.*

Shut. Up.

I am sweating. In fact, I have never been so sweaty in my entire life. I lick my lips and taste salt. I should be tired, but instead I am tingly to my fingertips, awake. It's like when I put on Shane's black shorts and Rachel's high heels, something happened to me. The shoes made my hips sway back and forth as I walked (well, almost ran) across the restaurant floor, and when I looked in the mirror and saw my makeup mask on—the black eyeliner, the red lipstick—I knew that Eden was right, that all I had to do was pretend to be someone else, someone brave.

Something clicked on the floor. I could only think about the things I had to do, things other people needed, and there wasn't room for anything else in my brain. Everything got squeezed out, and there was only me and this pounding, loud, explosive place. I did drop a tray of waters onto someone's back, and I thought that was the end, but when I glanced back at the kitchen, Fred was laughing. After that, it was butter.

Now I've mopped. I've wiped down counters and honey jars and the insides of refrigerators. I've covered lemons and limes and put away ketchup bottles. There is something about this that makes sense to me. There is a beginning to the night. There is chaos and running, and there are loud noises. And then the door closes, and when I'm done ticking down the list of side work, when all the boxes are checked, there is an end. The kitchen is clean. The floor is peaceful. Everyone is exhausted but happy. It's a dying down. Order.

And something else. I'm good at this.

And now I'm holding money, so much money, in my hands.

"Go ask Val to make that into twenties for you," Rachel says.

"Oh my gosh, thank you!"

"Don't thank me, love. You earned it," she says.

I made more than a hundred dollars.

Val has money all around her, and she counts out twenties, takes my pile of ones and fives and tens.

"You did good." Fred startles me. His apron is off, and without it he's just a nerdy-looking guy with suspiciously sharp teeth and dirty glasses. His hair is slicked back, and his face is clean. He is still in his socks and clogs, though. If you saw him walking down the street, you would never know he is commander in chief of this weird empire.

"Thank you," I say. There is something about Fred that makes me want to do a good job for him, and I feel like I just got an A on a test I thought I was going to fail.

"I think we're going to keep you."

My body aches empty.

"Yeah," Shane says, and she throws an arm around me, "I told you, Freddie. When are you going to learn to listen to me?"

He grins and pulls a cigarette from his pocket. "Val, you locking up?"

I text Eden to tell her I'm ready to be picked up, and when I get outside and look for signs of Mom's car, I find Digby sitting in his orange International, affectionately dubbed The Beast, and everything in me goes liquid.

I feel sorry in advance, since I am going to have to skin my best friend for this.

I'm freezing in this getup. Why didn't I put my clothes back on? I want to run, except I know that would be mighty rude, and it's cold and I don't want to walk home. So I try to look regular as I approach the car.

He pushes the passenger door open. "Hey."

"Hey." I get in, try not to squelch against the leather.

"Eden asked me to pick you up. Wren fell asleep, and she didn't want to leave her."

We take off with a little rumble, and I try not to look at his hands.

"Nice shorts," he says, and I hear the smile in it.

"I have to wear this."

"I never pegged you for a Fred's girl."

"Necessity is the mother . . ."

He shifts around. "They look nice. I didn't mean anything. The shorts look nice on you is what I mean. You have nice legs."

My turn to shift around in my seat. I pull at my clothes in hopes of covering myself up some more, then find out that short shorts have nowhere to go but where they already are.

"What I mean," he says, "is that you seem too shy for Fred's, and I have never really seen your legs before, and they are nice."

"Okay," I say, "no need to go overboard." Silence. Silence. "And thanks. And maybe I'm not so shy." I'm thinking about the night I just had. "Maybe you're the shy one."

He seems to mull this over. "Maybe I am."

We pull up to my house. It snuck up on me, came too quick.

"Would you grab Eden for me?" he says.

"Sure." I get out. Get a clear shot of his eyes, the sweet clean green he carries around with him like it's nothing. I force myself to stay with them, to see what's in them. Pooling lamplight is what. Wee sparkling stars. It's like that. He looks away first.

"Have a good night, Lucille." He says it like I'm standing outside the driver's-side window.

"Yeah, Digby." *Tink.* Snapshot. Him, just like that, turned away, I'm pretty sure because he can't look at me. "I'll go get Eden."

Eden is reading, legs splayed like a broken doll. Wren is crashed out on the couch.

"So?" She scans me head-to-toe from behind her book. Faulkner. "Damn, you look pretty good all tarty."

"Yeah? Good, because I was thinking I'd just go ahead and give up the Converse and the overalls as per your suggestion and wear this daily."

"How much did you make?"

"One hundred and eight dollars exactly."

"Not bad. Also, that's a sacred number. Portent. Good things to come." She slaps the book shut. "Digby's outside?"

"Yes." I try for a pointy look. "Thanks for the warning, by the way."

"Why do you need warning?" She's putting her book in her bag, not looking at me. "It's just Dig."

"Wren?" I ask. "Was she okay?"

"Oh, yeah. We did some rocking out, a little homework, watched *Cake Boss*. He made some kind of lizard." Eden yawns. "I don't know how he does that. It shot flames out of its mouth and grew new tails when you ate them. He's like a god." She gives me a quick hug, squeezes my shoulders. "Mrs. Albertson came by, though. She wanted to talk to your mom."

I thump. "What did you tell her?"

"That she's on vacation."

"Oh."

"What?" she says from so far away. "What's the matter?"

So many lies.

The Night That Was the End of Everything

The night Dad went away, I left the window open because it was getting to the time of year where it never really cools down but Dad hadn't gotten the air conditioners out of the basement yet. One of those choices I wonder about now. What if my window had been shut? What if the air conditioning unit had been on, whirring away? Would Mom even still be alive?

I thought Dad was a pig.

Dad was a mewling, snorting pig making noises outside my window, only I didn't know it was Dad at first. I sat up looking for the source of that awful, sickening noise, tried to figure out how a pig escaped from a farm somewhere and wound up in the middle of town. Then the pig said my mother's name, not once but over and over again, a squealing mantra.

"Lauralauralauralauralaura—" High-pitched. Animal. Not a man. Except it was Dad. My belly told me. The spit that filled up my mouth told me. My pittering-pattering chest told me.

"Shut up, baby," Mom hissed from down on the street. "Get in the house."

I shook in my sleep shirt, took short, quick steps to the window, and hunched down, but they were too close to the house for me to see anything. I stared at the quiet street, our neighbor Andrew's perfect bushes across the way, and listened fierce.

"I can't, I can't," he said. "I can't go back in there."

"Just—Tony, just walk five steps and get inside."

"It's all a lie. I'm a failure. I failed at this, all of it."

"You didn't. Who cares about a stupid raise? It's nothing."

"You made me care about this shit. This is your fault." His voice got louder, higher. "You did this."

"What did I do? What did I ever do to you?" She sounded so defeated.

"You wanted babies. I gave you babies. You wanted me off the road. I stopped playing. You wanted me to get a real job. I did it. You did this to me." He edged out, so I caught sight of his burly shoulders, his old Bones Brigade T-shirt, worn and falling over his chest, his belly, his hands in his hair. "Look at me. Look at me. I'm not a man. I failed. I have nothing to show for any of it. I should be surfing, playing music, not doing this soul-sucking crap. I can't do this anymore."

"Do what?" Mom's voice was so hollow and thick, I almost cried out to her then, but he went on.

"Any of this. I suck at being a suit. I'm a loser. You can see that, right? It's killing me, this whole sham of a life. *You* are killing me, all three of you. No career, no house of my own, I'm a nothing, a nothing. And you're a vampire." A low voice now, one I had never heard before. "You're a succubus. You and those fucking kids have taken everything from me." He pointed. "You did it on purpose."

"You can't leave," Mom said.

"Why not? You don't love me. I don't love you. What's the point?"

"I love you so much, I'm sick with it," my mother said, and I knew it was true when her voice cracked. He shook his head. "Tony, come in the house." Soothing now, like she was talking to Wren with a bloody knee. "Just come with me. Let me make you a cup of tea."

"Tea?" He laughed. "*Tea?* What are you, out of your mind? I don't want tea. I want my life back. I want what you took from me, dammit."

"Tony," Mom said.

That's when he grabbed her.

They stumbled against each other, and I pressed my nose into the mesh screen, trying to see them, but they had disappeared under the porch awning, and all I saw were the cars parked along the sidewalk. So still. It was so still for a second. And then they staggered back into view, Dad's hand on Mom's neck, dragging her.

Back to the pig noises, the snorting, squealing. He looked up. I don't know if he was searching for God or stars, but what he found was me. And I swear to you, I swear he wasn't there. A monster was. Dad's face twisted, his skin gray and dull in the lamplight. But his eyes, his eyes were on fire.

I spun and twisted myself out of my spot and down the stairs. I flew, I think. It's the only explanation for how fast I got out the door. And then I was on him, on his giant hand, yanking and prying. He let go, even with the monster in him, like I was a Taser, my skin on his weakening his grip. Mom fell to the ground, now making animal noises too. She puked a little while her breath tried to come back to her.

Dad's legs went out and he cried like Wren did when she was new. Worse than that, because something inside him had scattered, and I knew it right then. The police, the ambulance, they all came. Even a couple of volunteer firemen. It didn't take long for word to get out. After all, we live just a few houses down from the fire station.

Mom tried to stop them from taking him, even as her neck turned colors. She wouldn't press charges. He cried a long time in those flashing lights while Irv and Linda, the cops, tried to get to the bottom of things. At some point Dad started laughing, a hyena now, and they put him in the car, I'm pretty sure mostly because that laugh was such a nasty sound and nobody could get him to stop.

"Don't take him. That's my husband." Mom kept saying it, but they explained that they had to, at least for the night.

He wound up on suicide watch in the institution—sorry, *mental health clinic*—and that's the last I saw of him, writhing and growling in a cop car.

You'd better believe everybody came out of their houses after they took him too. It was like a damn town meeting. Andrew on his porch in his silk robe. Even Smoking Guy two houses down. Middle of the night, early in the morning, smoking, smoking.

Nobody said anything about it. Not to us. They just shuffled a little more than usual. *Sorry,* I wanted to say. *I'm so sorry we messed with your suburbia.*

It got to be morning while it all went down. As the cops drove away with Dad, Linda and Mom talked in the little alleyway in voices too low for me to hear. Birds tweeted happiness.

Mom tugged on my hand and didn't do much more than glance at the neighbors as we went inside. She pulled me up the stairs into Wrenny's room. Wren was still sleeping, of course, would stay still another couple of hours at least, her amazing sleep-through-everything powers at work. We slipped in on either side of her, collapsed onto the full mattress, pressed into her body, in the room that had once been Aunt Jan's guest room. We looked at each other over her head. Wren was an anchor between us and we held tight.

"Mom."

"Lu."

"Do you need to go to the hospital?" I kept my voice steady. "For your neck?"

"No, baby. Let's just sleep now. Only a few more hours before I need to go get your dad." She tucked a piece of Wren's hair behind her ear, wiped away some of the sleep sweat on her forehead. "Let's rest our eyes. There'll be so much to do when we wake up again."

"Okay," I said, wanting to ask her questions about what was coming, about what had happened. Was he drunk? On drugs? Would she really let Dad come home after what he did to her, after what he said about us? I already sensed that there would be a before and there would be an after, and that the divide happened when my father put his hands on my mother's neck, or maybe when he said he didn't love her. There is no real recovering from that, is there? Some things can't be unsaid, undone.

"Is Dad going to be okay?" I ventured in a whisper.

"Of course. We're all going to be fine."

Mom smiled at me then, little creases pinched at the sides of her mouth, and reached her arm across Wren to rest it on my side.

"He's a good man, you know," she said.

She sounded so desperate for it to be true that I had to turn over. I knew she wasn't smiling because everything was going to be okay. She was smiling because it wasn't, and there was nothing else for her to do.

Day 28 cont'd

Wrenny's face has angry couch imprints on it when I pull her book off of her chest, her cheeks flushed with pink sleep. She throws an arm around my waist, and we count stairs up. She never opens her eyes. She doesn't have to. This is her home, and her feet know the way. She's never lived anywhere else.

"One," I say.

"Two," she yawns.

All the way to thirteen. She makes a left.

"Where you going, Wrenny?"

"Mom's room."

"I think you should sleep in your own room tonight."
I mean, at some point this has to change, right?

She looks at me like I deposited my brain at the bottom of the stairs.

"I don't like it in there."

"Did you brush your teeth?"

"Yes," she says, and she looks me up and down. "Before I fell asleep on the couch."

"Okay," I say, like that's the reason we're going in Mom's room again, and not because I don't have the energy for arguing.

"You look like a rock star," she says, grinning now.

Like a trollop, I think. "Thanks," I say.

She runs a hand along my arm. "Sticky."

I do the same to her cheek. "Yeah, you too."

"And you smell like a burrito."

"Just keep the compliments coming, cookie."

"Well, you do. And maybe also a taco."

She makes straight for Mom's bed, the rumpled sheets left from this morning, all the rushing, no time to make it. She crawls in, watches me as I get undressed and reach for a towel. There's no way I'm getting into bed without a shower. There's a sound not unlike peeling Velcro when I take off the short shorts and tank. I wrap myself in the towel, then hold it open, let myself cool down.

"What are you doing?" Wren asks. "You're naked."

"I don't know what I'm doing." I cover myself. "That's a very good question, though," I mumble. I start to head for the bathroom.

"Are you leaving me?"

I stop in the doorway. There's something in her voice.

"I'm just going to shower," I say. "I don't want to get in bed smelling like Mexican food."

"Can I come?"

"Into the bathroom with me?"

"I don't know. I don't want to be by myself."

But I do.

"I'll sit on the toilet," she says.

"No, Wren, you stay in here." Clock says eleven thirty. She's going to be a mess in the morning.

"I could get in with you."

"Into the shower?"

Nods.

"Stay here. Sleep."

Her eyes fill. Jaw sets hard.

"You can wait for me in there, I guess."

I run downstairs and flip on the dishwasher, then take the shortest shower ever, just long enough to get soapy all over and rinse it off. As the hot water trickles over me and I am wishing for the motel water pressure I remember from going to gigs with Dad, I push my face into the tile. I wish I could go right through it, disappear into it, disintegrate and never come back. My shoulders shake, my face tightens, but I do not cry. I only press harder until my nose hurts and I think I might accidentally break it.

When I check on Wren, she's sleeping in steam, her eyes closed again, head against the sink, mouth open.

We are lying in bed together. I curl myself around her. She lays her head on my arm, and I hold her so tight.

I'm not sure anymore which one of us is more afraid to be alone.

It takes me about two weeks to get a groove on. Get up at five. Do homework. Get Wren and me ready for school. She takes baths while I do my work next to her and try not to get the paper wet. I walk her to school a little early, drop her off, then go myself. Charge through the day the best I can, pick Wren up from school, run home, cram as much housework as possible into the half hour I have, then run to work four days out of five. I have to make all the money I can.

I took a hundred dollars and bought myself three pairs of shorts, all black, and some matching tanks. Shane gave me a pair of her shoes so I didn't have to buy those, and my feet don't hurt so much anymore. I work from four until around eleven, then take my stacks of money home. I line up our bills in order of importance, get money orders from different places around town, and pay as I can. I have covered electric, gas, and phone so far. Better late than never, right? Still, as soon as I'm done paying one batch, more will come. Oh yes. They will come.

It's a thing now. Four nights a week, Eden drops me off at work in my car, and then when my shift is over Digby picks me up, then takes Eden home. Eden does homework with Wren so I don't have to worry about that, and when I get home Wren sits on the toilet while I rinse off, and I talk to her through the shower curtain, then we climb into bed together and cuddle up close until we both fall asleep.

I don't think about Mom except sometimes as I'm waking up, when the phone next to me starts bleeping and buzzing at me to wake up. I see her bright blue eyes then, no light in them, the way they looked just before she left. Whatever barricades I have raised against them are at their weakest. So I take a second. I breathe. I stare into those eyes and then I fold them up. Once because she left us, twice because she hasn't come back, three times I fold her eyes, until they are so small, they are just meaningless blue dots, and then I blow them away.

Day 49

Eden is waiting outside on the porch when I get home from work Thursday night. I twitch inside Digby's truck, hug my jacket tight around me. I told her not to do that. The neighbors might see. She's smoking, but doesn't get up when she sees us pull into the driveway, only takes another drag.

Digby mutters, "You know I'm going to be the one filling her oxygen tank when she gets emphysema."

"Yeah, or me."

"We can take turns," he says.

"You care about stuff." I nudge him.

"Whatever." He studies the steering wheel. "I'll take care of my business, always. Eden's my business."

"Let me go see why your business isn't moving." I get out, as always, with that feeling like something is missing, like my usual wave isn't quite good enough. It's because I want to put my lips against his, inhale him into me, take him with me. I don't want to say goodbye. Ever. No wave will satisfy. "Thank you," I say.

"Stop saying that."

"Thank you?"

"Or, actually, say it ten times right now and then don't ever say it again."

I giggle like a dummy and get out of the car.

"You owe me ten." He says it so seriously, I almost stand there at the window and do it, but then the side of his mouth turns up and I walk away.

"Chatty," Eden says.

I realize my cheeks hurt from smiling, and I force my face to relax. Gaw! What is wrong with me?

"I thought your fixation was cute at first, but maybe a reality check?" she shoots without preamble. "He has a girl-friend."

Digby's passenger window is open and I want to shush her, but I can tell she is in a mood. I don't say anything, but if the zipper on my hoodie went all the way up, I would pull it right over my face.

"What's the matter?" I say.

She crushes her smoke and waves away the last of the slinky fog. "Good news or bad news first?"

"Bad." My gut is a rock. What now?

I start pulling weeds from our little patch of grass to distract myself.

"I can't do this for you anymore," Eden says. "Babysit Wren."

I almost have money to pay the cable bill so Wrenny can keep watching her cooking shows. I try to imagine her life without them and I can't.

"I'm falling behind in ballet."

Of course she is. I hadn't even thought of it. She said she could only do two nights. I just buried it.

"I want to be there for you, but I'm not going to enough classes. I want us to be all with our riverside plan, except I can't and still do what I want to do with my life." She kicks the chair underneath her. "I don't want to let you down, Lu."

Her lip is doing a quiver thing. Not a good sign. "And all I can think is, if I'm this tired, you must be . . . And Wren is awesome. I don't mean that she's not—"

I drop my weeds, walk up the porch steps, and sit down on the bench next to her. "It's okay. I'll just have to figure something else out."

What choice do I have?

I get it. Madame Renee is terrifying. The few times I've seen her, I've wondered how she gets her bun pulled so tight that her eyebrows meet her hairline. I wouldn't mess with her either. And to be honest, I hadn't really thought that Eden's dancing would suffer because of me. That's the trouble with letting people help. It always costs somebody something.

My brain is running through possibilities and coming up empty. I don't have anybody else. I never expected Eden to bail on me, and I'm not seeing another solution. Instead, I am seeing Wren and me in frayed and discolored woolen blankets walking the streets begging for alms. We have dirt on our faces and under our nails, and we shake in the cold. Because in this fantasy it is sometime in the 1600s and I have an English accent.

Digby honks.

Eden flips him off. "Hold your horses, cowboy!" she shouts.

It's late for all this noise, and I can see Smoking Guy's cherry from here.

Eden's voice drops. "My mom is going to get a phone call from Madame Renee any day now. I don't know why . . . I don't know why I thought this would work. I wanted to be your hero. I thought your mom would come back." She throws her hands on my shoulders and we sit forehead to forehead. "What kind of person doesn't come back?"

"I don't know. What kind of person leaves in the first place?"

Eden pulls at the ends of my hair. "There are so many ways to leave."

Leaving is easy, I think. *Easier than staying.*

"Lu," she says, "I think you should tell. It's getting serious now. It's time for you to tell someone."

"She can't." Digby got out of the car, I guess. "So if you two are done making out, can we think logically for a second?"

Eden drops hands to her side. I pull back.

"Maybe the system isn't so bad," Eden says.

"It must be nice in the land of ponies and rainbows," Digby says. "The fairies and the leprechauns are such a treat."

"Shut up," Eden says.

"No, really, when you and the last unicorn land back on earth, let me know."

"People are good," she says, "sometimes."

"No," Digby says. "People have good *intentions*. Those are two totally different things. Someone is going to walk in here, and you know what they're going to see? Two abandoned girls, a dad put away—no offense, Lucille—one girl working in next to nothing—no offense, Lucille—to pay the bills, the house falling apart . . ." He looks at me.

"None taken," I say.

"No social worker is going to leave things the way they are." He leans against the porch railing. So close to me. "So she can't tell anyone."

"Even though she turns eighteen in July?" Eden says.

Digby gives her a look.

She turns to me. "Lu, have you thought about maybe contacting your dad?"

I don't know how to say that I don't know where he is, that I couldn't get in touch with him even if I wanted to.

"I'll do it," Digby says, after he watches my face for a

minute. "Basketball season hasn't started yet. I can watch Wren for you for a bit."

I almost fall over.

"But your mom . . ."

"I'm out with Elaine almost every night anyway." I try not to let that sting. "And she has some big debate thing coming up, so she's busy. I'll tell her. She'll cover for me, and my mom will never know the difference. It'll be fine."

"Ain't you a sweetheart?" Eden smirks.

"Well what, Eden?" He takes off his hat. Puts it back on. "You want me to sit here and do nothing while Lucille and Wren get thrown into the street? You think anyone is going to give her a break? They might get separated, or have to live in some juvenile center. I can help. So let me help, and don't give me a hard time."

"Okay," Eden says, tucking her knees underneath her bony butt. "It's a little more time, Lu, like he said. But it's just a Band-Aid. You have to figure something out. Something permanent, if she's really not coming back."

My bare legs are starting to goose.

"Which brings me to the good news," Eden says.

She throws open the door.

"Such flourish," Digby says.

"Come in the kitchen."

We stumble past sleeping Wren in a line. Digby ducks a little as we pass through the doorway. All the cabinets are open. They are full. Every kind of rice, soup, canned vegetables, couscous, barley, box after box of pasta. Cereals line up neatly across the top shelf. Granola, oatmeal, and on and on.

"Holy crow," I say. "Thank you."

"What?" They say it in unison. Very twin.

"You guys did this, right?"

"No!" Again, unison.

"Well then, who did?"

"Just take it, Lu," Eden says. "Gift horse. Mouth." Looks to Digby. "Right?"

"This is good news?" Digby says. "Eden, think for a minute. Think about what this means."

"It means the cabinets are full. And, tah-dah! That's not all." Eden pulls on the refrigerator door. "This."

The fridge is full too. I mean really, extra full. So is the freezer. Vegetables, fruit, yogurt for days and weeks, sour cream, cheese, tortillas, and ice cream, chicken nuggets, meat and fish, eggs, juice, and even some bubbly water. I have never, ever in my life seen anything like it.

"It's awesome, right?" Eden says.

"Do you not see?" Digby says. "This means someone knows. Someone who doesn't want you to know they know. It's weird."

"Quit being so cynical, Dig," Eden says. "She needs this. It's like she has a fairy godmother or something."

"It was like this when you got back here from dropping me off today?" I ask.

"Yup."

"That means somebody did it in the clear light of day," Digby says. "That means they knew how long you'd be gone, that you'd have Wren with you, that they had to hurry. It means someone has been watching. Closely."

"Well," Eden says, looking less gleeful.

"Yeah," Digby says, "it's troubling."

"I have to start locking my door," I say. No one in this town locks.

Digby leans against the counter. He is always leaning. "I guess this isn't exactly a hostile action. It's kamikaze generosity, for sure."

I'm overheating. I want everyone to leave. I need to think and I can't, not while I'm standing here staring at all this food, and not with these two redheaded swizzle sticks hovering over me.

"At least you don't have to worry about food for a while," Eden offers. "Although that is a lot of carbs." She kicks up her legs and scooches herself onto the counter. "Okay, so there's one more piece of not-so-great news."

"Really?" I say. "Did a wall collapse?"

"No. Wren came home with a note. Mrs. LaRouche wants to speak to your mom."

Everything in me contracts.

"Mrs. LaRouche was the best," Digby says. "You remember how she used to get us to be quiet?"

"Bum bum bee dum bum"—Eden sings.

"Bum bum," I answer flatly.

"I don't think it's a big deal," Eden says. "It's just . . ."

"Going to be challenging to produce a nonexistent parent."

"Right."

I cover my face. Count to three. Uncover my face. Nope, it's still here, still this earth, this life.

Eden's face scrunches. "Lu."

"What?"

"You have a bloody nose." Digby reaches for a paper towel from the new ginormous pile that has magically manifested itself on my counter. The expensive kind.

"There are tissues, too," Eden says, pointing to the living room. "And toothpaste, mouthwash, Q-tips . . ."

"Stop!" I can't. I can't breathe, and it's not because of the blood that is dripping over my lips. It is all happening at once, and I can't make sense of it, of any of it, and I want to laugh just like I heard Dad doing. It's bubbling right under the surface, and if I let it go, I'll never stop. When Digby pushes the towel against my nose, I grab it from him and bat at his hand. My chest goes in and out, up and down.

Eden stares. "Dude," she says.

I find the couch in the living room while I hold my nose, and they are shadows on me and I want them to go away, need them to go away so I can think. I've got numbers, so many numbers, doing Irish jigs on my head, and Mom, and her eyes they are big and so blue and so empty and they are all over me and my short shorts hot pants sexy shoes and makeup, and Dad who knows where, and a best friend who actually looks scared and everyone else and their perfect simple lives and me failing Wren all all the time and some Good Samaritan who knows and a love, a love who is standing right in front of me offering me his help and is so out of reach and I am so alone and I need them to go away.

"You're going to be okay," Digby says. He makes a move for my hand and I jerk it back. "All this is going to be fine."

"Go home," I say, and my voice is hard. I've never heard my own voice like that.

Neither have the twins, apparently, because they both look like I just smacked them.

I wipe the blood from my nose, will the bleeding to stop. I march to the sink, splash water on my face, wash my hands, try to pick the blood from under my crooked nails. I'm pretty sure the splashing makes my mascara run, but right now I am too pissed off to care, and I don't want to look in the mirror because I don't know who I will find looking back at me. Mirror smashing will ensue. Just in case the seven-years-of-bad-luck thing is real, I'm not messing around. I'm not that far gone.

Welcome to my life.

The worst joke ever.

They are watching me like they're not sure what to do. I go to Wrenny on the couch and put my arm under hers, scoop her awake.

"Shower time?" she says.

"Yeah," I say, make my voice quiet so she won't hear the hurt. "Shower time."

I start up the stairs. Twelve to go. I don't look back, but I hear the door close behind me, the Beasty rumble. Mad that they left, but I would have shredded them if they had tried to stay.

Once I have Wren upstairs with her head leaned against the bathroom wall, I go back downstairs, close the blinds that look out onto the street, turn off the lights, and lock the door.

Day 50

I go to the public library to email Mrs. LaRouche from Mom's account, since one of the things Mom took was Dad's laptop. The librarian doesn't look up from her book, just hands me the sign-in sheet and waves at me with her very long nails.

"Good book?" I ask.

"Yeah," she says, nodding me into the computer room. "It's a good book."

I type in Mom's password. Tonylaura1031. It's probably not the best password ever, but my parents met at one of Dad's shows on Halloween, and then Mom wound up magically having Wren on that same date however many years later. 1031. If you knew that one simple set of facts, you could get into just about any private Bennett business there is. Well, if you also knew the bank account number, that is.

Mom has 551 new messages. There's no sign that she's been on this email at all since she left. Some of the messages look important, so I scan the subject lines for a second. Mostly it's a lot of nothing. A sale at the Gap. Special deals on travel to the Bahamas.

I get to it. As Mom, I explain to Mrs. LaRouche that I work days and that I am sending Lucille in to discuss Wren after school and that she should feel free to pass along whatever information she needs to.

I wait.

I read some Internet news, which makes me feel a little guilty, considering that I have so much homework to catch up on and that a very nice-looking lady with way too many bags is waiting for my computer. Whatever. I still have thirty minutes. In that time I wander onto E! news and find out that the guy from the forthcoming zombie/werewolf/slasher movie slept with this girl while on that set, while his pregnant wife sat at home, and he's here to tell the world just how sorry he is. Not so long ago I could have told you all the celebrity news. Now I know nothing. Lately, it all filters as superfluous babble, but it's pretty nice right now, I have to say.

Just as my hour is running out and I'm about to have to turn the computer over to the lady with all the bags, a new email pops up.

Mrs. LaRouche will be fine having a conversation with Lucille. It will be delightful to see her after such a long while, she says. How about this afternoon?

I want to call Eden and tell her, ask her what I should do, how I should handle it, but I know I can't. Something bad happened last night when I made Eden leave, but I'm not sure what.

The classroom looks almost exactly the same as it did when I was in fourth grade. The book-cover posters have changed, but it still smells like apple juice and impending puberty. Wren is waiting for me on the playground with Shane and Melanie, and I can hear the kids shrieking out there.

Mrs. LaRouche is cute behind her desk, with her glasses hugging the tip of her nose so far down that I don't even know how they stay on. Her indiscernible chin has gotten even less discernible, and she wears a pageboy haircut that went out of style, like, thirty years ago.

"Ah." She scoots from behind her desk and proffers a bony hug. "Lucille Bennett. It has been a spell, hasn't it?" She's originally from Georgia, and the accent has stuck. Her teeth are yellower than I remember. Aging looks like it sucks. "Have a seat, please."

I do.

"You'll always be nine to me, I suppose." She gives me a head-to-toe that is only acceptable because she was once my teacher. "You are turning into a beautiful woman." *She said "woman" to me. Gross.* "How are you, sweetheart?"

"I'm okay," I mumble. "Senior year and everything."

"You're a senior?" Shakes her head. Her hair does not move. "What happens to the time? Do you have big college plans?"

I have no college plans.

"I'm thinking about a gap year," I say.

There is a definite uneasy pause, like she's waiting for me to explain myself, which I am not going to do.

"So there was something about Wren?" I don't mean to be rude, but being in this classroom gives me the heebies.

"Yes." Mrs. LaRouche startles back to the papers in her hand. "Of course. I'm sorry your mother couldn't come today. This is rather important, I think."

I will hold it together no matter what she says. I am strong.

"Yeah, her hours got all changed around. It's a mess. Some nursing politics." The nursing lie spins and spins.

"All right, well, she said it was fine with her if I share this with you, so let's talk."

"Okay."

"Let me begin by saying that your sister is a remarkable child."

"I know."

"She is far more developed than her classmates in a variety of areas. Science, for instance, and math."

"Oh."

"She also has excellent verbal skills. Did you know that Wren is currently reading at a ninth grade level?"

I should start reading out loud to her on my nights off. I should do a lot of things.

"Quite frankly," she goes on, "if it were up to me, she would move forward and skip a grade. She seems unchallenged by the curriculum, and she simply breezes through her work."

"That's all good news, right?" I say.

"Ah, well." Mrs. LaRouche removes her glasses and allows them to fall on their chain around her neck. She looks at me square. "Yes, all of that is good, but I do have some concerns."

"Okay," I say.

"Wren appears extremely anxious, especially recently." She hands me a paper.

I have a stomachache.

"She has requested lately to sit away from the other children. She complains that noise bothers her." She points to a desk in the corner. "That's where she likes to spend her time. She's rather good-natured about it, but she is isolating herself. I'm simply worried that Wren is disappearing into her own world, not engaging with the other students, and I'd like to make our school counseling services available to her, if that's all right."

"For what, exactly?" I breathe. In. Out. In. Out. "What good would that do?"

"There has been," she says gently, "a lot of change for Wren in the past few months." She sighs. "I really would have preferred to speak to your mother about all of this. It must be difficult for all three of you."

"We're fine," I say, then think of what an adult would want to hear. "We're in an adjustment period."

"Yes, well, I'd like to show you something." She hands me a piece of paper, Wren's writing all over it, the pink pen, the curly letters, the hearts over the *i*s.

"Should I read it?"

"Please," she says. "Take your time."

It says:

My Hero

My hero is the Barefoot Contessa. The Contessa bakes and she's round. The Contessa always has people over to eat dinner and we never have people over except Eden and Digby. The Contessa lives in a pretty house and our house isn't pretty. She has a soft voice and I bet her hugs are like pie. I bet she would tell me I'm pretty even though I'm not and that she would never leave ever.

I put the paper down. Mrs. LaRouche sits across from me. "Do you talk about this last summer's events within the household?"

I shake my head.

"I believe those events affected Wren much more than

she is willing to admit, and I'm concerned that if the issue is not addressed openly within the home, it will begin to eat away at her. She needs a place to express herself without fear of repercussion."

I nod.

"At this point, I would recommend some family counseling. There are some wonderful people who specialize here in town." She hands me a piece of paper with some names. "But if you don't pursue that avenue, it might be good for Wren to feel she has somewhere safe to discuss her feelings. Often," she goes on, "a gifted child such as Wren can unconsciously take on all the guilt and sadness associated with a situation like this." She reaches a cool hand across to mine. "There can be some depression, of course."

"She seems happy."

"Eventual drug use, violence, eating disorders . . ."

"Okay!" I say with more force than I mean to. "Okay," I say, softer. "I will tell my mom to sign these papers so Wren can talk to someone. We'll take care of it."

I want to get out of here. I want to run to the playground and squeeze Wren because she sees everything—is seeing too much—and I can't stop it or help it or help her. I want to pause everything for Wren, charm her into unconsciousness like Sleeping Beauty, and wake her with a kiss on the cheek when I have fixed everything.

"She seems to be connected to Melanie St. James a little. Do you know her?"

"Yes," I say. "We've played at the park a couple of times."

"Well, your mother might encourage Wren to explore that friendship. Could be helpful. You never know."

I nod.

"And you, honey?" She squeezes my hand, and I realize she's been holding it for a really long time.

My mouth starts to shake. I hope she will not ask me directly how I am doing.

"Yes, it must be hard for all of you, especially with your mother working so many hours, having to do it all on her own."

Ha. Ha!

"I was glad to hear that Wren didn't bear witness," she says. "But you did, didn't you? You saw what he did to her?"

My stupid, weak inside self has shrunken down to nothing and climbed out of this tiny desk and is holding on to Mrs. LaRouche like she is the only good thing on earth. I pull my hand free. I will not cry in front of this woman.

I make a move to leave. Smile as best I can. "We'll take care of Wren, Mrs. LaRouche. She won't be any trouble for you."

"She isn't any trouble, darling," she lilts. "She's just going through something. It happens to all of us a time or two in this life." She stands too, rests her hands on her ancient tribal-print dress. "I just want her to make it, to thrive. I want that for both of you."

"Thank you," I say, and I mean it. I want us to make it too.

"I'm so sorry you're sad, sweetheart," she says as I reach the door. "It really is a shame. You were such a joyful child."

After that, I need some time to think, and Shane offers to take Melanie and Wren for ice cream since it's Friday and she doesn't have to work. Neither of us does.

I haven't ridden my bike in so long. I get on the tow path and pump as hard as I can, till all my muscles burn and my lungs flap and struggle. It's flat ground and I pass some joggers, but pretty soon I've blown past everyone, past the rocks, past the town, and I'm jamming up the trail, sweating hard, watching as green whizzes by.

Thinking. If I forge Mom's signature on the papers, Wren will be asked all kinds of questions and someone could figure this out. It would be another risk. If I don't, Mrs. LaRouche will get more and more suspicious and we could be in danger anyway. There's no winning here that I can see.

I jump off my bike and park it by a tree. I venture a little ways into the woods and find a place to lie down. I've only been here about a minute when a great swooping thing circles, dives, and rips a branch off the tree directly above me. It makes a great cracking noise like a gunshot, blows the air apart. It all happens so quickly that I almost don't register that it's a bald eagle, a prehistoric, violent thing. A massive thing.

As I watch it fly away I wonder what it means. If there are such things as portents like Eden said, what could it ever signify? And then loneliness, brutal and merciless, wields wicked fists and my fingernails scrape at the dirt. I am so lonely that people in China must feel it rippling all the way through the earth floor. I lie back and stare up at the patch that used to be a branch, broken and beige at its severed arm.

I ride home slowly, and when I get there I sign the papers.

Day 53

I am on my third cup of coffee as I push through the high school doors Monday morning, and it's doing nothing except fraying my nerves. Ugh, English. Ugh, thinking. Ugh, walking. And oh gosh please no talking. I pause at my locker, balance the paper coffee cup between my teeth, and start piling the books into my backpack. No one talks to me. Eden isn't anywhere. I only see Shane, who gives me a little pat on the shoulder as she cruises by with her in-school friends. Our friendship doesn't really translate, but it's nice to know she's there. I don't have anything to say anyway. My mind is blank. I am not thinking about bills or

Wren or laundry or my suck suck suckish parents. Frankly, stupid hard life, I don't give a damn.

This bleary state is the only thing that explains how Digby sneaks up on me without me sensing him, since I am always on the lookout for him lately. I haven't seen him since I practically threw him out of my house. Eden either. She must be timing it that way, since her locker is right next to mine.

"Hey," Digby says, in that way he has, like he's not sure how to make words come out of his mouth. "You're here."

"Hey," I return. "Yeah, I am."

He lingers over me, close, but not too close. The hallway is emptying out as people filter into classrooms.

"I was having thoughts," he says, tucking his thumb under his backpack strap.

"Well, that makes one of us," I say.

"Oh." He shuffles a little. "Yeah, I bet."

"So, what thoughts?"

"No." He smiles, and I realize he doesn't smile very often. "I mean, I was thinking maybe if today isn't a test day or something, I thought maybe you would want to get out of here."

I feel a lot of things at once. The urge to run. The urge

to jump on him and see whether he would catch me or let me fall. I am clearly mentally unstable due to exhaustion.

"When was the last time you ditched school?" he asks.

"Friday," I say.

"Really?" His face tenses. "Yeah, I didn't see you around."

"But before that, never." I fake-cough. "I've been very sick with a fever and cough due to cold."

He pulls on my T-shirt with a thumb and forefinger. "Come on."

The bell rings.

"Where?"

"Uh-uh," he says, "you're going to have to trust me."

"Trust," I say.

"You can."

"What?"

"Trust me."

"Oh."

"So let's go."

I don't move.

"Now or never," he says. He pulls his keys from his pocket and makes a jangly noise that wakes up my feet.

⚡

We walk side by side out the front door. We do not see Shane or Eden or (blessed be) Elaine or any teachers. The universe is temporarily my friend.

I want to ask Digby about Elaine, to ask him why he is taking me away, if this is because he feels sorry for me because of my short shorts and high heels, or if it's maybe his way of calling a truce.

I don't.

I walk, thinking how nice it would be to take his hand in mine.

Oh, you of the clearest of greenest of eyes. Oh, wearer of perfect freckles.

You are going to make worm's meat of me.

We go to Philly.

He has a plan. He announces that if we are smart about it, we can see Independence Hall and the Liberty Bell and find the time to wedge in a cheesesteak before Wrenny gets out of school. He says "Wrenny," just like I do, and for a brief moment we are in this together.

I close my eyes in the passenger seat as he talks and let

cool October wind blow in my face. Digby is next to me taking me somewhere, and even though I think it is just plain weird that this is how my morning is turning out, when I try to think of anywhere I'd rather be right now, I cannot come up with one single place. Against all reason, I fall asleep.

When I wake up, we are in a parking structure, and it smells like oil and trash. Digby's watching me.

I hope I wasn't crashed out with my mouth open or anything.

"Oh good," he says. "I was worried your nap was going to throw us off schedule."

"You could have woken me up."

Shrugs. Says, "Come on, then. Let's go learn stuff. Tour starts at nine thirty."

Our guide is ancient. Her name is Mildred, which, think about it, when was the last time you met someone named Mildred? We shuffle into a room where she asks people where they're from. Switzerland, two families from Germany who don't know each other but strike up conversations and go "*ja, ja*" and shake each other's hands with vigor and commitment. There is a lone guy who says he's from

Colombia. An inner-city fifth grade class. Everyone coos. Mildred waits patiently and then shows us a video about the Declaration of Independence. Digby watches everything, everything, while I try not to watch him too hard.

I want to test. If I rub my elbow against his, will electricity shoot out of my face or something?

Mildred leads us from the dark room to Independence Hall, and we walk around. "Imagine this room full of men all making their cases, arguing. It is summer, and there is no air conditioning. They are in here for weeks." Mildred the Passionate. Mildred the Wise.

I like the Liberty Bell, the crack in it, all the stories about what it means and represents. Digby, my Digby, opens doors for me, guides me through swarms of people. He is exactly the same as he is on the court. He swishes in a really boy way. He's graceful, like Eden. He doesn't bang into people like I do. He navigates. Aims.

"Not much to do at the Liberty Bell, is there?" He says this after we have stood side by side in front of the bell for about five minutes in silence.

"Take a picture?" I suggest.

The tourists are lined up in front, the part with the crack, but he slips around to the other side, where it's empty.

"No one would know," I say.

"That it's the Liberty Bell?"

"Yeah, I mean without the crack, what's special about it? It's just a dumb bell."

"Just because the crack doesn't show doesn't mean it's not there."

"You know," I say, grinning like a twisted clown, I'm sure, "that's hella deep, Digby Jones."

"Well, I am deep." He leans his head to one side, and his bangs fall across his forehead. I am the Liberty Bell. *Clang. Crack. Clang.* "Take the picture."

I do. He looks silly in it. Not one one-thousandth of his himness comes through. I have located a flaw: he is not photogenic. I am overjoyed.

"Now you," he says.

"Oh, uh-uh."

I refuse until he puts hands on my shoulders and I am physically incapable of fighting him.

"Look a little to the side," he says. I feel my face flush and smooth out the front of my skirt. Another thing I pilfered from Mom's closet. "Smile."

I do. I am thinking about him, thinking now I will have a picture and he will be the one who took it and even if I look horrible, I will know we were together when it happened. Evidence just for me.

"There's something about your cheekbone." He hands me back my phone. "The curve of your ear."

"Ear?"

"It's dangerous." He laughs, but it's not a funny laugh.

I don't know what to do with that, so I pocket the phone.

"Excuse me, sir," he says to a guard who looks exactly like an actor I can't quite place. "Where can we get the best Philly cheesesteak ever?"

Guy points. "About six blocks up. They'll do you right. And if you're up for it, you can get a horse-carriage ride on your way. Very romantic."

"Oh no," Digby says. "No thanks. We're not . . . This isn't . . ."

"Okay, man," actor guy says. "Settle. I didn't mean anything. Just a suggestion. Take your Chevy-o-legs. Those work too."

As we walk six blocks, Digby points out a girl in a tiny skirt and says how she's wearing a postage stamp. He tells me how cityscapes are some of his favorite things. He says how he thinks American history is totally badass, and how he wishes he knew more but he doesn't want to do reenactments or anything, he's not that much of a fanatic. He pulls his phone out of his pocket when it makes a noise, and texts while walking. Elaine, I bet.

I'm trying to pay attention, but all I can think is how uncomfortable it made him when that actor guy thought we were together. I remember that Digby is a good person, a really good person. He's the kind of person who sees a girl in distress and wants to do something nice for her like take her for a day away from her troubles. He's just geeky enough to think that Independence Hall and the Liberty Bell are good distractions, and not risky like a dark movie theater or something.

Do you register that, backstabbing brain? He has a girlfriend. Someone he loves. Someone not you. Can you get that through your gray matter? I scoot away from him to put some distance between him and my thoughts.

So why did he call my ear dangerous?

"This is the real deal," he says as the guy makes our cheesesteaks. The guy in question is covered in tattoos, missing several teeth, chopping up hot peppers and onions, dragging slabs of steaklike substance around on the hot griddle. What is his life like? What does he go home to? Beer? A loving wife? A loving husband? Heads in his refrigerator?

"Lucille," the woman behind the counter croaks. Also missing some teeth.

I grab our sandwiches, and Digby reaches for the Cokes. We head outside, since it's lunchtime and there's no place left to sit.

"Here." Digby motions us to a stoop in front of an apartment building. We settle ourselves on it. "I like Philly," he says.

"Because of that?" I point to the abandoned building across the street from us. A couple of old guys are hanging out there, drinking beer wrapped in paper bags. I think how that's going to be me soon, probably.

"No," he says, and takes a big bite of his sandwich. Grease and peppers ooze out of the yellow paper it came in. "Because of that." Like it's on cue, a guy goes zooming by on a motorcycle. Hardly any clothes on, feet on the seat, doing a wheelie. He flies through the light with a huge grin on his face.

"That's insane," I say.

"Philly."

We eat some, and he looks at me sideways. "You know what I was thinking about?"

"What?" This is a really, really good sandwich. Even better since Digby bought it for me, and the Coke goes down with just the right amount of bubbles.

"The paintings you used to make when we were little."

I wipe away at some steak juice. This was the last thing I was expecting.

"What about them?"

"I was just wondering if you ever do that anymore. Paint."

Shake my head.

"Too bad. They were good. I mean, I remember thinking they were back then. You were covered in paint all the time. I remember my mom telling your mom to put you in overalls because you were ruining everything you owned."

That's where the overalls came from. I totally forgot. And the painting?

It's amazing what you can forget, even about yourself. I don't think I've picked up a paintbrush since I was nine years old.

"So why'd you stop?"

"I'm not sure. I just did. Grew out of it, I guess."

A breeze whooshes by, and even though it's a city street, it gets really quiet.

"You all right?" he says, finally.

"Fine." I put the sandwich down in my lap.

"I mean, after your mom, your dad, and everything?"

"I'm *fine*." It comes out so loud, I startle myself. "Jesus. I wish everyone would stop asking me that. If I'm not fine, I will tell you."

"Okay, okay." He scrunches up the yellow paper. "I'm just trying to be considerate."

"You can have the rest of my sandwich if you want it." A feeble attempt at peace.

"I'm a one-cheesesteak kind of guy, thanks." He shakes his head and his hair flops across one eye again. "I have a surprise for you."

Turns out there's a noon café concert just a few blocks from Independence Hall. He really did have a plan. So he takes me into the darkness after all. Digby Jones is turning out to be a very confusing person.

People are drinking beer and standing around, some are even dancing. It's Jupiter's Green Daisy playing today, and the band is so tight that I get thick in the throat. Dad would love this. This is home. I forgot it was. Music carries the weight of being human, takes it away so you don't have to think at all, you just have to listen. Music tells every story there is. This isn't the especially dancy kind. It's more of a swoon and I just take it in. I can't help but sway some, and Digby is so close to me, right behind me so I can feel him there. I want to lean back into him, but I don't. Then his fingers are on my arm again, touching light, tracing slowly, and my lungs are huge, bigger than they ever have been. I don't ever want it to stop.

Trace me forever.

In my perfect movie version of life, this is when he grabs me, turns me around, and kisses me. We are there in the inscrutable darkness, and the drums are beating inside us and his lips are on mine and he is breathing me in all hot. Not like the sad slobbery kisses I've gotten. Not like the dry sandpaper ones either.

The music stops and his hand drops and everything collapses. I tell him I'll be right back and I go into the bathroom.

Something is falling out from under me. Is it the earth? I stare at myself in the grimy mirror. I've been avoiding mirrors for so long.

You are so messed up, girl, I think at my reflection.

A woman with way-too-cool Manic Panic red hair is reapplying her matching red lipstick. I want to ask her if we can swap bodies. I want to run back to Digby and wrap my legs around his waist, put myself all over him. I want to ask him why he is doing this to me. I want to yell at him that he is screwing with me now, that he should stop touching me if he doesn't want me, that I am going to drown in him and I am already drowning. I force myself to look in the mirror again. Wren's right. I look like Mom.

The way home is pretty quiet. I have my window cracked, and Digby is playing music I don't recognize. The green blur outside looks like soup to me as we drive fast, faster than I want to, back to Cherryville.

"I know you don't want to talk about . . . things," he says, "and I really don't mean to upset you."

I pry my nose away from the glass and look at him. It hurts my eyes. He hurts my everything.

He glances my way, then looks back to the road. "But," he goes on, "have you given any more thought to the person who broke into your house? I mean, does it bother you? Because it bothers me."

"Yeah," I say, "I guess." One loose lock has fallen on his cheek, and I want to push it back. "It really wasn't you?"

"Nope," he says.

"Promise?"

"Look at me," he says.

I do. I do. I do.

"I did not put food in your house," he says. "I would tell you. I swear."

I want to cry again. It's like a reflex from hell.

"Hey." He puts a hand on my leg. "I'm so sorry. I didn't mean . . . I mean, I guess this is all a lot. And I would . . . I would have done all that if I had thought of it. But I didn't."

I swallow. Get myself under control. Stare at his hand. "I have been thinking lately that maybe there are just some things we can't explain," I say. "That maybe when a lot of bad things happen, good things have to happen too."

"Like magic?" He laughs, pulls his hand back, downshifts. "Come on, Lucille."

"Like balance," I say. I sound crazy. His face tells me so.

"Maybe," he says, and when he shifts again, the outside of his hand brushes against mine. "Maybe so."

He drops me off in front of Wren's school.

"So, we saw a woman wearing a postage stamp for a skirt, witnessed an almost-naked guy on a motorcycle, learned some history, ate some amazing food, and even went to a show, all in one day." He leans back against his window, and the truck rumbles like it's tired of sitting here. "Not too shabby."

"Yeah," I say. "It was good to get away." The maintenance man, Mr. Bob, is out front pruning the bushes. I remember Mr. Bob. Nice guy. "It was a good day."

"Sometimes it's hard to remember good days," he says.

"For you?" I blurt. "How can that be? Perfect family, perfect academic record, perfect jock, perfect girlfriend." I pull on my backpack. "Perfect face, perfect body." I reach for the handle so I don't have to look at him.

I hear him sigh, though.

"So I'll see you in an hour?" he says.

"You will?"

"For Wren."

"Oh, right," I say. I have to work.

"So I'll see you soon."

"Soon," I say.

When I am out of the car and almost to the courtyard where the parents and babysitters wait for the kids, I turn back. I want to say thank you for a perfect day, not ten times but ten thousand. *One perfect day with you is all I needed right now, and you gave it to me. You told me I had dangerous ears. You bought me a sandwich. You asked if I'm all right. You traced my arm again, and for three minutes I thought you were in love with me.*

But he's already gone. Still, I have a picture of me looking at him, and one of him looking at me. Two pictures just for me.

I am lost in a bubble, trying to remember specific things about this day, things I know I will want to be able to see clearly when I am lying alone in bed, later. Memories slip, you know, if you don't take the time to find a way to make them stay. How his shoulder blades jutted under his shirt in the back, how his hands shook for a second when he pulled the cash out of his wallet to pay for our sandwiches, how he paid really close attention to Mildred and said "Thank you, ma'am" when she showed us into Independence Hall. The music, the rush of it. His softer-than-I-thought fingers.

"How are things?" My across-the-street neighbor Andrew is in a houndstooth jacket, his nails clean, his eyes bright and shiny, a green umbrella in his hand.

I look up. Just the slightest chance of rain.

"Fine." I like Andrew, so I make an effort. "Everything's good."

"Good, good." He taps his umbrella on the ground. It's so pretty. Sturdy and new-looking.

"How's Amelia?" She's his daughter.

"Oh, she's fine. The usual things. Piano today, homework, and early to bed, I think." He runs a hand through his blond hair. Curls his mouth around clipped words, everything precise. "We're well into fall now, and it's time to get back to a routine."

I start planning a routine in my head, remember everything Mrs. LaRouche said to me, remember everything.

Andrew is watching me, so I try to plug back into our conversation. "It's nice," I say, "listening to Amelia practice piano through the window. She's really good." It's not true. She's only a little bit good. She's also eight.

"When Amelia was born," Andrew says, only partly to me, "we weren't sure whether or not she would have AIDS. Her mother had it, and it took us about a year before we knew for sure. She was also born addicted to crack. So the piano helps with her focus and concentration."

"You knew she was sick and you took her anyway?" Andrew has never told me any of this before. I remember when he and Edwin adopted Amelia, brought her home wrapped in a blanket. It just goes to show you never know what's happening behind someone else's closed door.

"Absolutely," he says. "We wanted a soul to take care of, and why not a soul in need?"

"Wow."

"And so I told myself that I want her to be able to do one beautiful thing. Just one. Whatever it is. I chose piano for her because it keeps her hands busy and she has to practice every day, and it is the one thing I know how to give her."

"One beautiful thing a day."

"That's right." He looks like he wants to say more, something about me, maybe, so I draw my hood up around my head and say, "I hope you guys have a good afternoon."

"Making beautiful things," he says, and winks.

"Right," I say.

Day 54

The next day, when Wren and I get home, the leaves in the yard have been raked, the flowers watered, the two bushes pruned. Two pots of mums, one persimmon, the other yellow, have appeared on either side of my porch. I should be grateful, I know, but I am so pissed off, I can barely take it. I approach my house like the walkway is a landmine. Somewhere, Wrenny is bouncing around, ecstatic.

She *loves* the flowers!

She *adores* the grass!

And *Look! Look!* Someone left a basket of potpies by the door!

Potpies? I think. *Are you freaking kidding me?*

"Sweet," I say, trying hard to stay steady. I grab the basket. My laser eyes settle on Andrew's house. This would be just like him, to be all perfect and Good Samaritanish, to notice more than he should. It must be him. But if he's milling about being a do-gooder, loading plants and food in and out of my house, someone is bound to notice, which means that it's just a matter of time before more people start asking questions.

I am just about to march across the street when I spy Andrew pulling up in his new Volvo station wagon. He gets out and pulls a Bergdorf Goodman bag from his car. He's dressed spiffy, as he is when he's been in New York. If he's been there all day, he couldn't possibly have done it. He looks my way and shoots me a thumbs-up.

"Nice work on the yard!" he says, with that combination of surprise and joy, like it's the oddest thing in the world that my yard would look pretty like everyone else's, but he's trying to be supportive. His hair is perfect even though a little wind is picking up. Soon it will be cold in earnest.

Who is doing this?

⚡

That night, after Wren falls asleep, I make my way into the attic. I generally stay away from that area. It's pretty grim. After Aunt Jan died and Mom was all swollen with Wren in her belly, she took everything but the furniture out of the house and shoved it up there. She never said anything, but I think she couldn't throw away Jan's belongings or give them away either. Right before she left, she did the same with Dad's stuff. All signs of him vanished.

Now that I think about it, that says a lot.

When I was little, I used to go up there by myself every once in a while, just to poke into my fears, I think. It creeped me out, and I liked being scared sometimes. I would go halfway up the stairs and imagine what might be lurking. A psycho-killer? A crazy lady ghost, with wild black hair and thin, cracked lips? Or spiders? A million-billion spiders just waiting to jump all over me and lay eggs in my face, hatch their babies all over.

Then I would flip on the lights, stare at all the boxes—nothing crawling anywhere, no threat. Just an alive sort of quiet, pregnant like Mom, filled up with something indefinable. Still, I could never quite get all the way up. I am remembering now what was under some of the tarps, and I want to get to it.

It takes me a minute to adjust to the light. Two of the fluorescent bulbs don't work anymore. All I see are outlines of boxes, and lots of guitars and basses. It's like I've got fingers in my chest pushing one by one, their tips trailing along my ribs, down my stomach. I'm doing something I'm not supposed to. I have entered the sarcophagus.

I don't remember much about my Aunt Jan. Nothing, actually, because I never met her. Mom left Cherryville as soon as she was old enough, headed to the West Coast. She says she followed the music. Their parents died in a fire, I guess, something tragic while on a vacation in the woods. Smoke inhalation. That was all Mom ever had to say on the subject. She would go glassy. Even in her softest hours, she drew some kind of invisible line at that story.

Mom had a picture of Aunt Jan that she kept on her shelf in the bathroom when I was really little and we still lived in California. At some point when she was pregnant with Wren and Aunt Jan was already dead, she told me that the baby and I would have exactly the same age-spread as she and her sister had. Seven years and three months apart. You have to wonder, don't you, about patterns like that?

Weird, she muttered back then, stroking her giant belly as she explained.

I sift through some boxes of clothes, some moldy books, some canvases that just about dissolve in my hands. Spiders do crawl around, and some other unidentifiable bugs. They don't scare me.

I get to what I'm after pretty quickly. I carry the yellow plastic boxes down the stairs, flip off the lights again, and then sit on the floor and open them. Paintbrushes of all widths, hundreds of tubes of oil paint, pencils of every kind, pens upon pens upon pens.

I take the paints out of the drawers in the boxes, lay them on the floor, line them up by color until I have a rainbow around me. My skin sizzles, my mouth a little dry. I open a tube, test it. Oil comes out first, but then a little squiggle of a gloaming blue spreads across my fingertips, and I rub them together. They tingle.

Day 61

I drive myself to work these days, since Eden isn't trying to hide out at my house anymore. I haven't talked to her in weeks. The arm that used to save me my seat in English is now an elbow and a hand that shields Eden's face from mine, telling me to stay away. I sit in the back mostly, since I'm always only right on time after dropping off Wren. She's ignoring me at lunch, too, face all in a book held straight up so I can only see her black, chewed-up nails and her pissed-off red hair. I've taken to sitting outside the front of the building on my own, staring at an uninteresting sky while eating an uninteresting sandwich. That has never happened before. Not ever. My chest is cavernous, emptied of her. My personality too. Empty. I don't know who started the not-talking thing and I don't know how to end it, so I don't do anything about it. I endure instead.

Digby keeps showing up nights, though, parks the Beast right in front of the house where Janie could drive by and see it anytime. He doesn't seem to care, so I don't say anything. And Elaine? I never ask about her, but I guess she knows where he is all the time. He will deal with his mom if it comes up, he says, and I believe he can, will. Something about him gives me faith, even though I know that Janie Jones would go psycho bananas if she knew what was going on around here. That lady would choke my mom herself. She's the kind of mother who would lift a car above her head for her kids, and I know she would at least wrestle a badger for me.

"Honey, I'm home," I say to Digby when I get in from work. He is lying on the couch doing something with his phone. I plop myself down next to him, still sweaty and smelly and too tired to care. "Where's Wren?"

"She fell asleep in front of the TV upstairs."

"By herself?"

"I sat on the stairs so I'd be right there if she needed me, but yeah."

"That's a miracle." It really is. "Thank you."

"Don't sweat it." He sits up. "You must be tired."

"No." I don't want him to leave yet.

I close my eyes, though, can't help it, but it's not from sleepiness. It's because he's kind and generous and gives for free. He can't be real. My bellybutton is grateful. Even my knees are grateful for everything he's doing for me.

He's staring at me. I feel him through my lids. I open my eyes and really look at him, force myself not to shy away. I am not expecting him to be contemplating me like he's trying to get to the bottom of a really long math equation. A wave of pain rushes over his face. I catch it as it zaps his eyes, his mouth, as it tackles his insides and his stomach twitches under his shirt. I know that pain like I know his loping ways.

I expect him to get up like he usually does, start packing his bag, but he doesn't.

"Your yard looks nice," he says.

"So they tell me," I say.

Touch me. Kiss me. I'm yours. Yours.

I know he won't, though. He would not cheat.

I like his shoes. Vans. His long feet.

"Nothing else has happened, right?" he asks. "Any revelations about who's doing all of this?"

"Can we not talk about that, maybe?" I don't want to talk sad, because if I start, everything will push in.

"Okay." He puts his phone in his pocket. "Do you want me to go?"

No. I want you to stay forever, you major bleeding moron. "Don't you need to?"

"I have a little while," he says.

I pull off my shoes, grab a blanket and throw it across my lap.

"I'm smelly."

"A little. But it's a good smell. Makes me kind of hungry for delicious burritos of every flavor." He rubs his perfect belly and grins. "So, was your night good?"

"Uh-uh." I shake my head. "You," I say.

"What?"

"Talk about you. You always ask about me and don't say a thing about yourself. It's kind of totally unfair."

His cheeks brighten, redden again. It's cute.

He shrugs.

"Not good enough," I say. "I think you're an avoider and a deflector. So tell about you."

"Not like you answer my questions either."

"See? Avoider," I say.

"You know everything about me," he says.

"Definitely not everything."

I want to make him blush all day.

"Favorite food," I say. "Start with that."

"Really?"

"Favorite food," I repeat.

He bites at his own lip. The top one. "I like salad."

"Salad?"

"Yes," he says, like he's admitting he wears girls' underwear on occasion. "I like salad. Fresh field greens, okay?" He's grinning that grin I love.

"But that's so unmeaty."

"I know," he says, "I think that's the point. My mom is always making a ton of food, right? Mega meat and potatoes. Pasta and roast and chickens and — I don't know. It's a lot of bulk and carnage."

I lean forward, pull my toes out from under me. "Digby Jones, are you a secret vegetarian?"

He turns a little to the side so we're facing each other

more, kicks off his shoes, puts his feet up onto the couch. They are mere millimeters from mine. "I like that you can do so much with things that come out of the earth. But you know I like my steak, too. As long as it's in Philly."

"Well, anyway, it makes a weird kind of sense."

"In what way?"

"I don't know. You seem . . ." I choose my words carefully. "You seem too sensitive for meat."

His hand jumps toward me for a second, then backs down.

"Do you want to know my favorite food?" I ask.

"Nope. I know it."

"You do?"

"Yep. Well, I mean, I know what it was."

"Well?"

"Bell peppers."

My body stutters. When we were younger, while everyone chomped on chips and drank Kool-Aid, I always went for bell peppers. I don't know why. Something about the crisp, the juice, the simplicity. I haven't had one in so long, though. I haven't just sat down with a plateful of pepper slices and let the clean taste of them freshen me up.

"Paying attention, Digby Jones," I say.

He breaks eye contact.

"What?" I say.

"Nothing." He takes off his hat, holds it between his hands on his lap. "I like it when you say my name." The tiniest wrinkles tickle at the sides of his eyes. "So are peppers still your favorite food?"

"I don't know," I say. "I don't even know *that*."

He totally rolls his eyes.

"What?"

"Everything is so dramatic with you lately. *My mom left me with my little sister. Some guardian angel brings me stuff. I work in a restaurant and have to actually talk to people.*" He gives my feet a little smack. "*Wah, I have even lost track of my favorite food.*"

Coming from anyone else, it would be mean-spirited. From him, it is somehow not.

"Are you finished?" I say.

Shakes his head, eyes all on me again. Mischief. "*Wah,*" he says, "*I am so beautiful. Wah.*" He slows down. "*I am smart, I am competent, I am making the impossible possible.*" Barely audible. "*I am amazing.*"

"Amazing," I repeat, but I am saying it about him.

"Yes, amazing. You did a crazy thing that night, with your dad."

I start to protest.

"I know you don't like to talk about it, but you jumped on—what?—a two-hundred-and-thirty-pound man and wrestled him off of your mom. I mean, that was really . . . amazing."

"It wasn't like that," I say.

"What was it like, then?"

"I don't know. He didn't fight me. He let go of her as soon as I touched him. It was like he didn't know what he was doing for a minute, like there was something else controlling him."

"Temporary insanity."

"I guess not so temporary."

"And you haven't seen him?"

"No," I say. "He wouldn't see any of us. Mom tried a bunch of times, and then finally . . ." And then I say it out loud. "He disappeared too. He's not at the clinic. My mom found out right before she left. I don't know where either of them are. It's like they evaporated."

He rubs my foot some, shakes his head. "I don't know how anybody leaves you, either of you. But especially you. I don't get it."

His hand is still resting on my foot. I am a giant foot,

his hand a magical giant hand, and it is all over me. Breath. Less. Whole body warm and throbby.

"What are you doing?" Who is this boy I've known for most of always, and why is he everything?

He smiles, and I swear, I swear his eyes are wet. "I don't know." He does not take his hand from my foot.

I crawl. I fold myself over myself and I crawl over to him, annihilate all rational thought, everything that is telling me to stop, that what I am doing is wrong. I pause when I get close.

Then his hand is on the base of my back and pulling me onto his lap. I rub against his slippery jock jacket, take his hat from his hands and let it drop. I run my fingers down the white stripes on his chest. Wimpy shallow breaths escape my lungs.

The air that comes out of him is sweet, and I take it. The tips of his fingers push. I hope my air tastes as sweet to him. The very edges of our lips touch, and shock after shock zaps me. My eyes are open and staring at his closed lids, and then they snap open and we are so close that he is a blurry Cyclops. I am sucked into his single eye.

"Lucille." He whispers it like a supplication.

We kiss for real then, and I don't implode or dissolve or

fall all to pieces like I thought I would. I expand into deliciousness instead. We sink into each other. His lips are soft and his body is hard and grasping, and after we test each other's mouths for a minute, it's like we are the hungriest people on earth and someone has just served us to each other for dinner, for dessert. We're steak and mashed potatoes with a side of gravy, and chocolate molten lava cake with whipped cream and raspberry sauce. We are decadent. No. He is a crisp, fresh, cool piece of pepper going down. Perfect, like I said.

Which is when his phone vibrates on my leg and I jump back. It goes and goes and goes. His face says he knows it's Elaine calling. He doesn't answer. He doesn't move at all. It vibrates forever before it finally stops. Another few seconds go by, and then it vibrates again. She left a message. What did it say?

Maybe *Hi, it's me. I love you, Digby. I miss you. Where are you? Call me when you get this.* I can almost hear her voice. What would she do if she knew her trustworthy boyfriend was all over another girl, and if she knew it was me? How would that make her feel?

I scoot all the way back, lean myself against the couch's

arm. He looks like he has just lost something. He will run away now. He will leave and never come back.

He pulls on one of my sweaty toes.

"Lucille, I—"

"*Wah*," I say, "*I am gorgeous. Wah, I have outrageous physical prowess. Wah, I have a beautiful girlfriend.*" I pause, try to get myself even.

His voice is salty, like I stole everything sweet out of him. "I'm confused, Lucille. This ridiculous girl I have known forever is what?" He rests his head in his hands, stares at the floor. "Is she interested in me? Is she curious? This girl is incredible. Her eyes, Lucille, you should see her eyes." I have to hold on, literally grip the couch under me, to keep from sliding myself back onto his lap. I don't even know this person I am with him.

His phone buzz buzzes. A text this time.

"Don't you need to get that?"

"No," he says. "It'll be all right." Snaps out of whatever we were in. I am jolted. After a minute, he says, "So what's going on with you and my sister?"

"I don't know." Why is he asking me about this now?

"You're not talking, right?"

"Not really."

"You threw her out," he says. "She was trying to help."

"I threw you out too," I say. "You're here."

"But—"

"But what?"

"I couldn't help but come back."

"But she could," I say, trying not to think too hard about what he just said.

"Well, you should talk to her. I think her feelings are really hurt."

"I'm sorry," I say, "I don't have time for all the feelings. I'm just trying to get by." It's only when I say it that I realize how fragile I am, how pissed off at Eden, how I don't think it's fair that she should have her feelings hurt when I am dealing with everything I'm dealing with.

"I have something." He pulls his phone out of his pocket. "Give me just a second." He quick types something that I assume is a text to Elaine while I try not to feel the sting of it, and then puts the earbuds on me. It softens me up that he does that, even though Elaine lurks between the notes. "You're going to like it."

The music isn't like anything I've ever heard, not my

usual for sure, but I like it enough to close my eyes. When it's over, he has his hat on, his backpack on his shoulders.

"Good, right?"

"Yeah, good." I hand him back his phone. "Thanks." Everything hurts as he goes toward the door.

He hugs me so tight on the way out. I try to press myself into him, and for a crazy second I think if I hold on tight enough, maybe I will actually become him, fade into him and none of this will matter. But in the end I am still me and he is still him, and our bodies come apart and his hand is on the doorknob, his backpack on one shoulder, the night on my face.

Then nothing.

BDWC
(Before Dad Went Crazy)

Parker Delaney is the farthest I've ever gone in the sex realm. Seems like forever ago now, back when I had Mom and Dad and I didn't know how breakable everything is. I still thought you get a family, some clothes, a best friend, a sometimes-annoying little sister, and you go about your day until you get old enough to see what the world is really about.

I used to spend afternoons at the park with Eden sometimes, when we still lived side by side, before Mrs. Albertson moved in. We would watch the boys play basketball—hoops, they said—and we would lie on the spinny merry-go-round, stare at the sky, talk a lot of smack.

Parker wasn't my boyfriend, but he was as close as I ever got, in that he was kind of regular about wanting to kiss me. It had been that way for a long time. One day I wound up behind the karate dojo right across from the park with Parker's hand up my shirt, down my pants. So many things happened at once. Thoughts about whether or not I liked him, about whether or not it mattered, his tongue too wet, too big, not giving me the chance to catch up to it. His hands, too. He must have had eight of them, sprouting everywhere at once.

He had this really soft hair. I wanted to run my fingers through it, to spy into him and see if anything was there, to talk to him some, but he was moving like he was going to catch fire if he didn't get as close to me as he could. It was like he had a bomb in his pants that was going to go off and explode the world if he didn't get what he wanted, if I didn't let him touch me. I had to pry myself away that last day, or I would have lost my virginity against a dirty wall, and I wouldn't let him move me to a second location when he said his parents weren't home and we should go there. He promised he wouldn't push me, but I knew better. The brakes don't seem to work so well once you get past a certain point.

Kind of intoxicating and sickening at the same time.

I still had all my clothes on, but by the end of it Parker had touched me everywhere and I couldn't even tell if I really liked it or not. After Dad went away and until Digby, I didn't want to touch anyone, anywhere, and it sure as hell seemed like no one wanted to touch me.

I thought Digby was safe.

Day 61 cont'd

So after Digby is gone, I take the hottest shower in the universe while Wrenny sleeps in Mom's room, which means I can take my time, languish, feel the water in beadlets, think about that kiss, those kisses, brand every second into my consciousness. Remember what I said about forgetting things? That's real. You have to focus to keep things near.

Then I get into one of Dad's old T-shirts. It says WHY ARE YOU WEARING THAT STUPID MAN SUIT? That's a line from *Donnie Darko,* Dad's favorite movie.

Digby's hands were so soft, but something about the

pressure of his fingers on my back sent me flying. I'm thinking how lips so close but barely touching made me feel romance-novel things. My thighs they quivered, my breath it came quick, a moan escaped. Like that. I crawled, for chrissakes, crawled onto his lap like a wanton creature.

I also didn't hurt. For a few minutes I was exactly where I was, and truth? I would not have taken a million billion dollars to get off that lap right then. But now the pain is worse than it was before. So much worse.

I want, I want, I want.

Digby all over me.

I wish I could talk to Eden.

I can't stay still, have to move. I am up and running for the yellow box, for the warped but clean canvas I found. I pull it open and get the brushes out, the paints. This color, that color, I am in a frenzy. I cut the paint with thinner and I go to town on this canvas. The paint is a living thing. Orange, red, yellow, and then blue and purple and green all up against each other. I don't have a picture in my head. I only have a feeling about what it could be.

When I'm done, it's a tornado of color. I am absolutely

one hundred percent certain that it sucks by any real artistic standard.

But I know that the red, the orange, the yellow? That's me, burning. The blue, the green, the purple? That's Digby.

We are together in that painting, suspended.

Day 62

I go to Eden the next day. I can't get what Digby said out of my head. Are Eden and I fighting for real? I'm not sure, and I'm suddenly not okay with it if we are. I get to English early so I can sit next to her. I try playing footsies with her and find her unresponsive. I text her a love note during precalc, and she never responds. I even sit with her at lunch and have a one-sided conversation. That goes over so well, she calmly picks up her lunch and walks away while I'm midsentence.

She really is mad at me.

Day 67

Digby comes over as usual. There are no kisses. There is no touching. After he leaves, I find a red pepper, sliced into strips arranged symmetrically, on a plate in the kitchen.

Day 69

"I'm going to be a rainbow for my birthday!" It's the first thing Wren says as I walk in the door from work, carrying a couple of bags of birthday supplies in my hands.

She has on some faded leotard with big red, green, blue, and yellow stripes zipping across the front of it, and she is smiling so hard that I don't laugh. She is totally jacked up. I can't believe it's eleven o'clock. I drop the bags in the kitchen. Admittedly, I stomp a little.

"I hope it's okay that she went in the attic," Digby says. "She saw some things you brought down, I guess." He comes in behind her. "There's so much cool stuff up there. Boxes and boxes. There are all these guitars—" He stops. Assesses me for a second. "Sorry she's awake. I know it's a school night."

I made almost two hundred bucks at work, just in time for Wren's birthday. I should be in a good mood, but I'm mad or irritated and I don't know why. Maybe it has something to do with the fact that Digby and I haven't talked about how we kissed and he keeps coming back and I have to not touch him and it's holy hell torture, and now he's just going wherever he feels like going in my house, into places I'm just discovering myself.

"You're mama's so fat, I ran out of gas driving around her," Wren says, skipping in a circle.

"I'm sorry if you don't want her up there," Digby says. "She kind of insisted."

I take off my jacket and hang it up, try to get a grip and get away from them so I can calm down. Wren looks like she's having a manic episode or something. She has now paused and is sipping some chocolate milk.

"You shouldn't be drinking that this time of night," I say when I get back to the living room. "No wonder you're so wired."

Digby takes the milk out of Wren's hand. "There's all

kinds of artwork up there. Your aunt's, right? Do you still have any of yours from before?"

"Hey!" Wren says, and takes back the milk. Digby comes over to me.

"You should check with a person before you go poking around in all their personal things," I snap.

Digby gets that look like again, like I hit him, and I suddenly want to. Really hard.

"Anyway"—Wren flits between us, drinking once more—"I found this box of stuff. I know you said I should get cre-a-tive for Halloween since it's my birthday time, and so I thought I could be a rainbow." She pauses. "Maybe you could get me some glitter tomorrow, like, in the morning before school? I saw some that was all different colors. I could just put it everywhere, and if you get me some purple tights, I'll be almost all the colors."

"Wren, would you please calm down!" I yell.

I'm instantly sorry, even though Wren is acting nuts and Digby is too, a different kind of nuts, like he didn't cheat on his girlfriend with me, like there's nothing between us and he's just my babysitter. Digby and I stare at each other. It's a standoff and I am ready to shoot.

Wren looks back and forth between us. "I want to know what you think about my rainbow idea."

"Rainbows are magical." I break away from Digby, run my fingers through Wren's hair and come up against a huge knot. She pulls away. "And you are going to be the best one ever."

She twirls. "Halloween-slash-birthdays are the best. Remember when Mom and Dad dressed up like Shrek and Fiona?"

"You cried," I say. "Dad scared you when he came out with that mask on."

"I don't remember that," she says, looking deflated. "I just remember thinking it was cool."

"I was there," Digby says. "That happened. Sometimes you remember things differently from how they really were."

"Revisionism," I offer.

"Or perspective," Digby says. There's a pause. Then, "I have to go."

"Okay."

"Listen," he says as he pulls his keys from his pocket. "I don't want to stress you out, but Elaine's debate event was tonight. I don't think I can watch Wren for you on Halloween.

I wanted to do the trick-or-treating and everything with Wren, but now Elaine wants to spend some quality time together."

"But I told Fred I would work, even though it's a Friday. You said—"

"I'm sorry, Lucille, but—"

"No, it's fine, you should do that."

"Maybe we can both watch Wren for you."

The effects of this statement cannot be exaggerated. Vomit. Bile. Splat. I don't know how he can suggest it.

"No, thanks."

He squints a little. "Yeah, okay. Well, I'm sorry." He smiles and it looks so weak to me.

"Say it ten times and then never say it again."

"Lucille—"

"You owe me ten," I say. Then, "Wren, it's time for bed." I grab the chocolate milk out of her hand, huff as I walk into the kitchen, and throw what's left into the sink.

"Why did you get so cranky tonight?" Wren calls. "Cranky sucks."

"You know," I say to Digby from the kitchen doorway, "now she's going to be up all night. You don't give kids sugar before bed."

"I didn't. She just took it."

"Well, you're supposed to be in charge. In control."

"Like you?" he says. He sounds mad now.

"Upstairs," I say to Wren, who doesn't argue. "Good night, Digby. Enjoy all your quality time."

"I saw the painting," he says to my back.

I am taken down by sudden panic.

"I liked it," he says. "A lot."

"Me too!" Wren says. "I want to paint. Can we paint together?"

"Not tonight," I say.

"But—"

"Not tonight!"

Digby is still standing by the door. This is such a mess. The whole thing. And now I've hurt his feelings and he is trying, trying to make amends. I can see it. I can't leave it like that, don't want angry words between us.

"Go upstairs, Wren. Brush those teeth."

Shockingly, she does.

As soon as she's gone, Digby throws an arm around my waist and pulls me toward him in a fierce bit of hug. I hug him back really hard.

"You're trying to make me crazy," I say into his chest.

"I'm not."

I have to crane my neck to see his face.

"I'm trying to do the right thing." He runs a finger over my ear. Looks like he might maybe cry. "Can you get that?"

"Yeah, I guess." I move to touch his hand. He backs up so I can't.

"It really is a good painting," he says, and walks out.

Wren and I watch *Cupcake Wars* and I try to settle down. The teams are competing to throw a party for George Lucas, so the whole thing is *Star Wars* themed. We disagree about who should win. For me it all comes down to personality; for Wren it's flavors. She will root for a total bitch if she's making pistachio cupcakes with white chocolate frosting. Secret ingredient? Rose water. Wren is so excited about her rainbow leotard that I let her fall asleep in it, and me, I don't have the time to shower and change either. We pass out in Mom's room with the TV on.

Day 71

It's Wren's birthday. And Hallow-een. Something about that is gnawing at me. Like, we all wear masks all the time, right? And the fact that I wish so much that I could take mine off and come clean to the world, today of all the days, seems ironic on a level I can barely grasp.

Yes, I want to shout, *my dad is crazy, my mom left me, my best friend won't talk to me, and I am in love, desperately, never-to-recover, twisted-up sick in love with a boy I can't have. Go ahead, world, do your worst. I want to be free.*

I made a banner last night and hung it up in the door-way to Mom's room so it would be the first thing Wren sees when she wakes up. It has birds all over it, and a sun, and even a butterfly. It's a lie, of course, and Wren could probably have done a better job with it than me, but I tried.

Mom has a waffle iron that makes little heart-shaped waffles, and sometimes she would pull it out on a weekend morning and sing along to music while she cooked. It was always going to be a good day if it started like that. I find the pan behind the plastic juice pitcher, behind the metal platters that only came out at holidays, and I stare at it for a while.

It's only six in the morning, but I couldn't sleep. I had the phone next to me all night, just in case. If there was ever a day that Mom was going to call, it's today, and I want to be ready. I plan to very calmly pass the phone to Wren. I won't yell. I won't tell her bitter truths, and I definitely won't cry.

I want Wrenny to have a good birthday. She's ten now. Double digits.

This freakin' waffle pan is my nemesis. Just looking at it makes me tired. In and among the many things Our Patron Saint of Dry Goods left us was some pancake mix, so I crack it open, get flour all over me, and stir in milk and eggs while I let the waffle iron heat up.

The wind beats against the windowpane. There was

something Dad always did in the basement so the pipes wouldn't freeze. He would clean out the oil burner too and winterize the windows. If it's this cold at the end of October, it's going to be a rough one, and I don't really know how to do any of that stuff.

This looks almost like a normal morning, though. Coffee drips, waffles get golden, I set the table, and I get my gift to Wren out of the closet, down from the shelf where I've been hiding it. That girl gets into everything, so it's in the way, way back.

"What's that?" she says as she slumps to the table with a blanket around her shoulders.

"Happy birthday!" I say way too loud and far too perky, stick the box in my pocket. "You're ten!"

"You made Mom's waffles?"

"No, I made *my* waffles." I reach into the cupboard for the Nutella I bought, get strawberries and whipped cream from the fridge. "Did Mom ever do *this*?" I squirt whipped cream everywhere, all over Wren's plate.

Wren is decidedly unbouncy, even at the prospect of whipped cream, like she majorly came down from whatever high she was on the other night. Even though she is so sturdy, she looks infinitely breakable. Dark circles under her eyes.

"What's up, Wrenny?"

She shrugs, runs her fork through the whipped cream, gets some on the blanket, lets the fork fall back onto the table.

"I have something for you." I pull the box from my pocket.

Her face stays dull. It's so unlike her that I get tingly. She unwraps the gift like she's moving through sludge, puts the tissue paper to the side, the extra-sparkly ribbon that I thought would make her so happy.

"Did you see the banner I made?"

"Yeah," she says, "thanks. It's pretty." When she takes off the top of the box, sees the tiny diamond studs sitting in black velvet, she stares at me with huge eyes. "Are these real?" she asks.

I nod. "Of course they are." I don't tell her they were on superextra sale at the mall jewelry store. I want her to think I spent a million dollars. I would if I had it. For her.

"But we don't have any money."

"You're ten, Wrenny. That's a big deal. Anyway, they're perfect for you."

"But you're always saying how we need food and stuff."

I have done the wrong thing again. She shouldn't be thinking about these things. She should be frolicking somewhere instead. She glances at the phone sitting next to the stove, back at me, back at the phone. And then I know. She's waiting too.

"Your mama's so fat, I thought about her and she broke my neck," Wren says, before I can mention anything about anything.

"Why do you do that?" I put the strawberries back in the fridge and close the door a little too hard.

"Do what?"

"Tell those jokes."

"Because they're funny."

"They're not funny. Not really."

"What do you mean? Don't you get it? She's so fat, just thinking about her breaks your neck."

"I get it, I just think it's messed up. And it's not . . ." I search. "It's not kind." *It's not kind to yourself,* I want to say.

And then she's crying, big, globulous, full tears, crying all into the waffles, holding on to her own greasy hair like she's trying to keep her brains in place.

"It's still early, sweetie," I say, all the fight draining out. "She could still call. She has all day."

"I have school," she says into her hands. I hug her, but she makes a fort of herself. Wren has not cried through all of this, not once. How many smiles has she plastered on her face, and why are we all so busy trying to look okay when we're not? I get on my knees, force my face through her arms. She pushes me away but without much strength, and I am an inch away from her. I stick out my tongue and cross my eyes.

She giggles and I giggle back. She lets me part her arms and rest them on my shoulders. "We're going to be fine," I say. "Everything is going to be okay."

"Are they going to take me away?" She has never asked me until now.

"I would never let that happen."

"What about if you can't help it? I heard."

"Heard what?"

"You and Digby and Eden worrying about it. The night you got mad at them."

What else has she heard? How much does she know about any of it?

"I'm ten," she says, and I see how much she has changed, aged. The layers of happiness and carefree peel away.

"You are." I sit on my butt, so she is above me. "You are ten." I pull the blanket a little tighter around her legs. "So, do you want to talk about what's going on?"

Shakes her head but then looks out from under hopeful lids, long, thick black eyelashes. "I don't want you to get sad if I do," she says. "I know you get so sad." Her lip quakes, and I see how hard she is trying to make it stop. "I make you sad."

"No!" I say. "No. You don't make me sad at all, ever." I take her fingers into my own. She has the most beautiful nail beds. Perfect. Round. Pink and smooth. "Sometimes I don't think I do a good job," I say. "I make me sad. The situation makes me sad. And I like that you *seem* happy. But, Wren," I say, "if you're not really happy, you don't have to pretend. It's hard right now, but things won't always be this way. And I promise—promise—I'll take care of you, always." Something surges hard. "No matter what, I will never, ever let anyone take you from me. We'll be together as long as you need me."

"There's a lady at school who's been asking questions. She's really nice, but she asks about Dad and Mom and stuff.

I don't know what to say." She covers her face again, and I have to pull her hands away. "I haven't told her anything," she says.

"But you want to."

"I can't," she says. "She wants me to talk about my feelings, about what it's like in the house."

"Oh," I say. I'm not sure what to do.

"I think if I don't talk to her, it will be worse, but I think she's smart and she'll know if I lie to her."

"Well, then, don't lie. Just don't tell her everything."

"She told me it's okay to be sad too. But I am going to try to be happy anyway." She takes her free hand and pats the top of my head like I'm BC. "The earrings are really nice." She hands me the box. "Will you put them in for me?"

I sing "Happy Birthday" as I push the studs into her earlobes, and I can't believe how beautiful they are on her, like little reflections of everything she has inside her. I don't ever want that light to go out.

She stands up and looks at herself in the mirror over the sink. Our eyes meet. "Your mama's so fat, she's on both sides of the family."

She laughs like she's ten billion years old.

⚡

Shane and Rachel and Val are all over Wren right now, admiring her Halloween costume while they do their side work, cooing over her, telling her happy birthday every chance they get. Fred, who is dressed in full war regalia, double bandoleer across his chest, headband and everything, puts a candle in a flan, and everyone sings to her.

I hide my phone in my apron even though phones aren't allowed on the floor. Just in case. The girls take Wren into the office. When I check on her, they are doing her hair, making a huge deal over her earrings, asking her about boys. The restaurant is almost ready. Wren is mooney-eyed, sucking up every word they say as I roll silverware on the plastic-covered tables.

I love it when that's my job. Take the clean silver and roll it into napkins, make neat, tight little wraps and press them into each other. I can rest before the madness. And also, it's pretty how they look before they are unrolled and covered in muck. When I almost have a full tray done, Wren emerges from the office looking like a daytime hooker. A very happy daytime hooker. Apparently the girls refreshed her makeup.

"Whoo-hoo," Fred hoots, busting up when he sees her face. "Oh, man. You girls are crazy." He shakes his head and wanders back into the kitchen.

"Said the pot to the kettle," Val offers to his back.

"Look!" Wren says. "Rachel did my makeup!"

"Doesn't she look awesome?" Rachel rests a hand on her hip. "I accentuated her features, her natural cheekbones, those big lips." She holds Wren by the chin, gazes into her eyes. "Such a pretty face. Such a pretty little rainbow."

Wren does look awesome in a way that pulls at my chest. She looks too old to be just ten, and the black Rachel put around her eyes only makes all her hurt shine in her big sweet browns. I'm glad she's letting it show some. The red on her lips shines too, and I can see just how gorgeous she's going to be one day. I hope she will love herself so much. I hope she will know that she is beautiful without all that color on. I want to wipe it all off, but it will insult Rach, so instead I nod.

"That's right. You're stunning, Wrenny," I say. I put my arm around her and lean down. "But you don't need all that."

"I like it," she says, and struts back into the office.

Shane pokes her head out, applying lip gloss. "I told Rachel not to use the red," she says.

I shrug. "It's Halloween."

"You on the other hand," she says, "look like a freakin'

ghost. Is that what you were going for? Because if not, maybe a little blush?"

"What do you want for dinner?" I call out after Wren, ignoring Shane.

"Steak," she pipes back. I write up the order and slap it onto the counter by the kitchen window. I feel funny asking for the most expensive thing on the menu.

"You on some kind of protein diet?" Fred says, poking his head out and fingering the paper. "Gah-lutin free, perhaps?"

"For my sister."

He grins, pushes his glasses back on his nose. "Well, I guess since it's her birthday. The little queen needs her beef." I want to jump through the window and hug him. So many restaurants would never feed their staff steak. We get to order anything we want off the menu. I love Fred for that.

"Let's rock 'n' roll!" He shoots at me. "You look hot as hell."

Everyone tumbles out of the office tying aprons over their costumes. The people have gone all out with feathers and masks and face paint. I have settled on a black cocktail dress and a little of Wren's glitter. I do feel extra sparkly.

Wren is looking at pictures on the wall. All of us hugging, laughing, being silly. People are always taking pictures around here.

"You be okay?" I say.

She nods.

"I'll bring you your food when it's up." She nods again. "I'm sorry you have to be in here on your birthday."

"Why?" she says. "This place is rad."

No trick-or-treating. No friends for a birthday party. She gets to sit in an office her birthday night.

I pull on my dress a little, then head over to yank the dangly cord on the Open sign and have a minor nervous breakdown. There is already a line down to the corner. Val is at the door tonight.

"This is crazy," I say.

"They come from far and wide." She smiles. "I almost forgot you've never worked a Halloween." Val, who is dressed like a devil Betty Page, picks up a stack of menus. "Let them in," she says. "And I'll see you on the other side."

The night is mad. It's like we're the only party in town and everyone got the memo. I get a few minutes to check on Wren every once in a while. Once when I go in the office, she's eating, pulling bits of gristle off her meat and dropping them on the side of her plate, looking like some kind of really festive Viking attacking a feasting table. Another time I go in, she's drinking a soda. I don't know how she got it. When the night hits its peak, I find her dancing to the music on the floor. Finally I go in and find her slumped in the chair, her head on the table, looking uncomfortable and contorted. Some birthday. I have to get a side of guac for table nine and a check for table twelve. Usually this should not be interrupted, but I hate how she looks. "Tired, Wrenny?"

She lifts her head. At some point in the night she reapplied the makeup, and badly. Now she looks like she should be in *Rocky Horror,* as a rainbow transvestite. "So tired," she says. "Can we go home?"

"Put her in the car," Shane says. "When your section clears, you can go. I'll take care of the rest. We're dying down anyway."

I check the front. It's true. It's almost ten and we're about to close. It's still mayhem, but at least tables won't be turning over anymore. Everyone will be going to their next party, the real party. Everyone except me.

"Throw the heat on in the car and let her fall asleep in

the back," Shane says. "She looks like she's trying to pass out in an airplane seat. Poor little baby. I'll get your side work."

"Really?" I say. The side work at the end of the night is so long. There's mopping involved, and lots of bleach.

"Yeah," she says, "get your ass out of here. I'll bring your tips to school Monday." She pauses, rubs her fingers together. "Well, most of them, anyway. Gotta take a little cream off the top for mama."

She would never actually do that.

I lead Wren outside and lean her across the seat, put both our jackets on top of her, and turn on the car. It is so nice to be outside in the cold and the quiet after hours and hours of running.

"Lock the doors and stay down," I say. "Just go to sleep. I'll be done in fifteen."

I run back in, deliver the guac and the check to my now semi-irritated customers, apologize to Rachel, and then start praying for everyone to eat and get out fast. I tell myself this is a nice little town, that people don't get murdered here, that Wren is safe and warm in the car, that really there's no better place for her and no one will see her anyway, certainly not kidnap and dismember her or anything. I grab the credit card from twelve, run it as fast as I can, and search the floor for Rachel so I can turn it in to her to take back to the waiting family sitting there. Their kids are falling asleep too.

Which is when I smack into Digby like he's a damn wall and almost fall down in my silly high heels.

He is turning colors looking at me.

"What are you doing here?" I say. "I thought you were out."

"I was . . . am out. I just came by to check on you."

"Well, you don't have to. I'm fine."

"But it's Wren's birthday," he says, like that should explain his presence, like it has anything at all to do with him. "I pulled up next to you in the back. The car was on. I thought you might be out there. Wren's in the car."

"I'm aware of that," I say as snappishly as I can manage. "I'm just finishing up. I'll be out of here in a few minutes."

"Hey," Shane says, eyeing Digby, "I need to get by you."

"He's leaving," I say.

"No I'm not."

"Isn't your girlfriend waiting for you?" I spit. We're yelling a little bit anyway, the music is so loud.

"She went ahead to Parker's with Katrina," he says. "Eden is outside with Wren."

I want to cry. Eden isn't talking to me — she doesn't get

to talk to Wren, either. Also, if not for all this insanity, I would be going to Parker's too. I was there last Halloween. My biggest worry back then was whether or not he was going to figure out a way to defile me in my bumblebee costume.

"Move," Val says. She's not as diplomatic as Shane. "You two are blocking the way." She grabs a couple of beers out of the fridge. "These are for table six, Lucille. Make sure you tell Rach. Now beat it."

I march into the hall by the bathrooms so we can talk more privately, since it appears he's not going anywhere.

"I should have watched her for you," Digby says when we're alone, music beating behind us instead of all over us. "And it's her birthday and everything."

"She's not your problem."

I didn't mean that the way it sounded. Wren is not a problem.

He pauses. "Did your mom call?"

I shake my head because I can't manage anything else.

"Write? Send a present? Anything?"

"You should go," I say. "I want to get out of here and get Wren home."

He's shifting around, and him there, so uncertain and

vulnerable, it sends me into that trancelike state. Still, I try to hold my ground.

"Why are you here, Digby Jones?"

He gets a faraway, pained look on his face.

When he doesn't answer fast enough, I say, "I have to get back to work. I need to finish up."

"You look beautiful," he says. "Really."

"Go away," I say, but weak.

And then he's hugging me, his head leaned down into my neck. I am hugging back, and then my legs wrap around his waist like I've always wanted to, my back against the wall, and he kisses me again. So soft. So, so soft. This time it's different, not like finding out something new, but like returning to something perfect and familiar, to a home I wish I had.

"Shit," he whispers against my lips. I couldn't have heard him, he said it so low. I felt him say it instead.

"What the fuck is this?" It's Fred, and he looks like he's ready to pull out his fake guns and go out in a blaze of glory.

Digby takes a step back. I put my feet down. I am throbbing everywhere.

"Freddie," I say.

"We just got done seating for the night," he says, and I can't stand the look on his face, like I disappointed him. "You're not done yet. Get back on the floor."

"Okay," I say.

"I've got Wren," Digby says, and he scoots past Fred without meeting his eyes.

When I get outside twenty minutes later, Eden and Wren are playing Coca-Cola, standing next to Mom's car, slapping hands, wagging hips, smiling huge.

Coca-Cola went to town
Diet Pepsi shot him down
Dr Pepper fixed him up
Now we're drinking Seven-Up
Seven-Up got the flu
Now we're drinking Mountain Dew
Mountain Dew fell off the mountain
Now we're drinking from the fountain
Fountain broke, that's no joke
Now we're back to drinking Coke

Eden and I used to love that one. Whoever was quickest on the draw got to give the other a smack. They go for each other's foreheads now, and Eden lets Wrenny win. Takes the hit like a champ, smiling.

Eden catches me standing there, and I can't tell what she's thinking. I can usually read her so well, what with the brain sharing and all, but lately it's like she erected a Great Wall at the halfway point between us. It's funny how when you've done something wrong, or you're fighting with someone, they become scary, unfamiliar. Even though I've known Eden forever, even though she's my best friend, will always be my best friend, she is scary right now. She's scary because I'm afraid she doesn't love me anymore.

"I'm sorry," I say to her.

Eden shrugs.

Digby leans on the car.

"Thank you," I say to both of them. "For watching Wren. Again." Digby isn't looking at me.

"Happy birthday, Wrenny girl," Eden says, and gives Wren a big kiss on the cheek. "I'm going to get you next time, though."

"You'll never win!" Wren crows.

Eden glides her hand across my shoulder, then gets in the truck. "Come on, Dig, you don't want to leave Elaine over there too long. She'll have kittens." It seems like she said that to hurt me.

"Okay," he says. "Happy birthday, Wren. I'm sorry we didn't get to hang out today. I'll take you trick-or-treating next year. I promise."

"Really? Cool! I'll be eleven, you know," she says, and clambers back into the car.

He lingers.

"Why are you doing that?" I say. "Letting her make plans with you like that. You're going to make her hope."

"I didn't mean to. I will take her next year."

"Really? Coming back from college to take your sister's friend's sister to get candy?"

His face goes slack.

"Dammit," he says.

"She doesn't need to lose anyone else, get it?"

"Yeah, I get it," he says. "I'm a blockhead."

"Yeah, you are." A lying blockhead.

I think he's going to slink away, that I made him feel that bad, but instead he comes closer and drapes his arms around me. I shiver everywhere, so caught between the wanting and the hurting that I don't think I'll ever get away. I hold on tight, tight, only vaguely thinking that people might be witnessing us doing strange things, that anyone could be driving by and see us.

"Stay warm tonight," he says. "There's supposed to be an ice storm coming."

"Yeah, okay," I say. "I'll do my best."

When he climbs into the Beast, Eden watches me through the window as they drive away. She watches me hard.

I'm almost all the way home, Wren singing, wide-awake again after seeing Digby and Eden. My phone starts humming on my lap. I completely forgot to take off my apron. My heart totally vomits out of my face. I pull over and yank the phone out from under a bunch of straws and napkins. I don't recognize the number.

"Mom?" I say as I answer. Wren shoots up straight and silent. I wouldn't be mad at Mom. I only know it now. I want it to be her so, so much. There's a pause, a shaky voice on the other end. My insides drip away.

"Oh," I say. "Hi, Daddy." His scratchy voice rumbles at me.

"Your mama's so fat," Wren sing-songs from the back.

Day 72

I go to the halfway house the next day, even though the ice storm Digby talked about came and coated everything in premature winter, like translucent blown glass. The big trucks salted, and the roads aren't bad. The sun has come out a little, and it is melting everything away.

It doesn't smell so different from the elementary school when I walk through the doors that say COLUMBINE HOUSE, minus the apple juice and plus the off-center. If I designed a place like this, there would be little fountains, soft plushy couches, deep colors, not cheesy paintings on the walls. There would be things to fall into, against, to lean on.

Dad's been living here, in this house. While I do battle out there, he's getting up and brushing his teeth and talking to people, probably going to group therapy, lamenting how we ruined his life. What's it like to have everything stripped away like this, to just be a guy with a room, a bed, a roommate? Maybe it's a relief not to have to think all the time, to go sit in circles and talk about things or to listen to other people talk about their problems. I would take lots of naps. I would read all those books Eden always talks about. But what does he do? Maybe he's getting religion or something.

There are so many things I haven't wondered about until now. I've been too busy worrying about Mom, Wren, Eden, Digby. And here, this whole time, Dad's been forty-five minutes away. I never once thought of running to him. I wouldn't have known where to go, and anyway, after the last time I saw him it didn't seem like there was much to run to.

"What's your name, hon?" The house manager's Philly accent is thick, and her coarse fingers tug at my pinky. I wonder if she's been talking to me for long.

"Lucille," I say. "Lucille Bennett." I observe her very

large, flower-laden bosom. How did she get to be in charge of this place? Flowers on her dress, flower ring, matching flower necklace, fake flower in her hair. Seriously. Five more minutes looking at that and *I* will be insane. "I'm here to see my dad," I say.

"Get out," she says. "You're Tony Bennett's kid?" She appears friendly, but she looks precisely like a tropical version of the witch I had nightmares about when I was little, and now she lets out a cackle to match. For the fortieth time since I drove up, my conscience is eased about leaving Wrenny with Shane.

I nod.

"Well, I'll be damned," she says.

"Yeah," I say.

"Tony Bennett," she chuckles. "And he sings and everything."

"Hell of a coincidence, isn't it?" I say, and however it comes out makes her reach for the phone.

"Does your dad know you're coming? He didn't mention it to me."

"Yeah." I am empty space. "Well, I mean I told him I would try. He told me these were visiting hours." What if he doesn't want to see me today? What if he was just in some kind of mood when he called? I have not thought this through.

"Okay," she says. "Give me a minute. I'll get Carlos for you. He's my right-hand man. He'll take you to one of our meeting rooms." I must look alarmed, because she follows with "You'll be okay. Everybody loves your dad. Good guy. You're lucky."

"I am," I say. It feels like a question.

The floor is beige, with chairs to match. It's like they know there's no hope here and they've decorated for the occasion.

Every step I take, I get a little more emptied out until I am filled up with nothing, a head made up of ten thousand balloons. I can't feel my heart or my stomach or my lips. This is what surreal feels like. The guy who takes me back has a swagger to him, and even though the people who pass us titter and comment as I walk by, they don't get too loud. I think this guy is the reason.

". . . Carlos," he finishes. "If you need anything, you just call my name. That's what they keep me around for. It'll be all right, though. Your pops is cool."

The room is the size of a broom closet. Same sickly colors and uncomfortable chairs. I size up the room, then pick a chair so my back is to the door. Dad never sits with his back to a door, especially here I bet. I want to push off looking him in the face for as long as possible.

He wasn't ever a regular dad, you know. He wore leather jackets. He loved bands like Fishbone and Bad Brains, and when pop music came on the radio he acted like someone was personally trying to mess up his day. He drank beer on the porch while everyone else drank wine. He swore. A lot. The door clicks behind me. I don't move at all.

My father sits down across from me, and the first thing I think is how good-looking he is. I forgot his big brown eyes, his hollowed-out cheeks, how massive he is, his shoulders. How much like Wrenny. How little like me. He looks kind of old, though. There's gray in his beard scraggle. That's new.

"Hey, Tigerlily." He's the only person who's ever called me that. Because I'm part animal, part flower, he says. He lays one hand over the other, then taps out a little beat on the table.

I'm not scared of him like I thought I might be.

"Hey."

Eternity lives in pauses.

"So," he says, leaning forward finally, "how are you girls? How's your mom?"

"You haven't talked to her?"

"No." He leans back again, knees spread out wide, eating the space around him. He obviously doesn't know anything. "I haven't," he says. "I've been trying, but her phone says the mailbox is full."

"She tried. Before. A lot."

"I called," he says.

"You told them not to tell us where you were."

"I needed some space."

He *tip tap taps* on the desk again, and it's like *BING BONG BONG* inside my head. Everything is a million times a million in here. Magnified.

"I called," he says, then, "when I could."

When he could what? Face me? Face us? Face that he put his hands around Mom's neck and he *dragged* her. Why the hell am I here?

"So, your mother —"

"Yeah?"

"She okay?"

"Yeah," I say, "she's okay." What am I going to tell him? And does he really care? He said he didn't love her. So what about me, us?

"Are you guys okay for money? I mean, did she get a job?"

"At a restaurant."

He nods.

My mother. Nurse/waitress/who knows what. It's cool. His denial is working for me right now.

"So everyone's good, then?"

"Sure. Totally. It's a damn Unikitty party at home."

He lets out the most awkward laugh ever, and it is bigger than the broom closet. "I guess that's a stupid question, hunh?"

"Kind of," I say. "But that's what you want to hear, isn't it?"

"And Wren?"

"What about her?"

"Well, what's she doing?"

"Starring in the school play. She's taken up macramé and the flute, and on weekends she figure skates."

"Come on, Lucille. Really. Is she okay?"

"She's fine," I say. "Getting big."

"She didn't want to come with you, though, hunh? Laura either?"

"Guess not."

"Yeah." He leans all the way back in his chair and slouches down, dips his head back, and considers the ceiling. "Yeah, I guess that makes sense."

"It makes sense for sure," I say, even though Wren would die if she knew I was here.

I look up too. There are yellow spots everywhere in the popcorn mess up there. They should try covering them with some of Eden's smart words. Or they could make up their own, maybe. Troubled people have a lot of interesting things to say, and that's who lives in halfway houses, right? Troubled people.

"Man," he says, still staring at the ceiling, "you're being a little tough on me. You know I'm doing the best I can here, right?"

I can't help but stare at his hands. They are so big. Hands to hold you and swing you high above his head, to blaze across the strings on a bass, to force the reckoning in the music, hands that guide you and make you safe. Hands to hurt. Powerful.

"So, why are you living here?" I ask. "Why didn't you come back or go somewhere more interesting?"

He drums on his own chest. "I'm not ready to go back out there. I don't think I'm strong enough yet. I had a nervous breakdown. This was an option they gave me, and it seemed like the right one. I know it's hard to understand—"

"No, not at all. I mean, how nice for you."

He lets out a whistle whoosh. "Come on, Tigerlily, start over with me." His eyes are trying to show me he's safe. "Let's go for a walk."

It's such a ridiculous suggestion that I agree.

"Can you just walk around?"

He snickers. "Sure. I'm not on lockdown anymore, you know. I'm just under supervision. Got rules. But yes, we can go for a walk."

As we head to the backyard, he checks in with Carlos, who pads a few steps behind us.

"You know what the worst thing is?" he says.

"Hmm?"

"They won't let me drink in this place. It shouldn't be a big deal, but it's almost enough to make me want to break stuff sometimes. There are days when I'd give almost anything for an ice-cold beer."

"Nice, Dad."

"Look, I'm sorry to disappoint you, but you get your priorities straight in here quick."

I think he's trying to be funny, but I've got no patience for it. I brake. My feet skid on the floor, and I turn just before we get to the doors that lead outside.

"What?" He puffs up his shoulders. "What is it?"

"That's your priority?" I have to keep myself from lunging at him. "You think you get off with a few questions about how things are at home and then it's okay to talk about beer?"

His eyes ignite, then water down. He's off balance. I see him trying to smooth his fiery parts. I don't care.

"What is it, Tigerlily? Something going on?" He dares a hand on my shoulder. He's trying to corral me and it pisses me off. "You can talk to me."

He looks like a man, but all I see in front of me is a little boy. He has no right to that.

"Don't you touch me," I say. "Don't you put one hand on me."

He drops away. "Hey, relax. I'm just trying to take

my daughter for a walk, my daughter I haven't seen in five months. That's a long time. I missed you."

I can't hear that. He's twisting everything around to suit his reality, somehow making this my fault. When I think of all the times Mom came back from the clinic crying because they had turned her away, and for him then to not even tell her where he was going . . . I stride over to Carlos.

"Why is he in here?" I demand.

He glances around. "For the calm. It's a good place to get your head straight."

"Really?" I say. I swing back to Dad, who is watching me from the doorway. "I don't think you're all that agitated. I think you're weak, and I think this whole thing is a sham. It's a cop-out."

"I know it's hard to be here," Carlos says. "Maybe you should come back when you're less emotional. It's no good for people to hear yelling. Triggers."

"Yeah, yeah," I say. "I know. Calm." I take a breath. "You're right. I'd like to go now, please."

Carlos starts to lead me to the front, but I turn back to Dad.

"Go to therapy for real," I tell him. "Figure yourself out. Figure out how to tell the truth, take some responsibility.

What you did to Mom, the way you treated us, the things you said, none of it was okay."

He grimaces but doesn't say anything.

"And you know what else?" I say. "While you're at it, grow up."

Day 73

The next day I hover over my phone all afternoon. I pace. I pull pots and pans out of cabinets and then put them back in a different order. I start texts to Digby. I'm sure he could help me make sense of everything that has happened. And then I think, what if he's with Elaine, what if they're cuddling or something.

But I need.

I need something. I scroll through all the people I might be able to call. I keep coming back to Eden. Eden. Eden.

She touched my shoulder. Maybe I can call her. Maybe she's not off-limits anymore.

Wren has been in a funk since she talked to Dad. I only heard her half of the conversation, but enough to know he didn't say any more to her than he did to me.

What he said. What he didn't say. What *we* didn't say.

I'm usually happy when it's a Sunday, since I don't work and all I have to do is focus on the house and my homework, but today is gloomy, heavy again. I go so far as to touch all my paints, but nothing wants to come out.

Finally, shaking, I tap a few words into my phone and hit send.

It's done, I tell myself. Even if you don't get a response, you hit send and so now we'll see.

Mom never called. She didn't miraculously appear at the door. She missed Wren's tenth birthday. Wren won't talk about it, no matter how I try to keep it all open like Mrs. LaRouche said to. I think I was making her more miserable pushing the issue, so I finally dropped it and we watched TV all day long. I know how to make a whole bunch of family-friendly meals now.

We both fell asleep to the sounds of *Iron Chef*.

And now Eden has woken me up. She answered my

text. I steal out of bed, dig in Mom's closet for a pair of jeans and a long-sleeved cotton shirt.

Maybe, maybe I am forgiven. Maybe she is going to yell at me, for Digby, for everything. It doesn't matter. I'm not alone either way.

I fly to Eden.

Fly.

I say silent prayers that Wren won't wake up and be scared, and then I sprint toward the river. I am sweating under my jacket, running, running in the cold, past the naked trees and all the familiar doors.

The Beast is parked on the sidewalk by the entrance to the tow path. Did Digby come with her? My whole body thumps.

Once I'm off the path, I slip some. The black ice hides against the dirt, and even with the full moon I can't see it. I'm glad I wore my big fat snow boots.

The train car is so close now, and before I see her I smell a cigarette.

⚡

"You drove?" I ask. "I saw the Beast."

"Yeah," she says, flicking. "He's not here."

"I know," I say with too much in my voice.

She points her smoke at the moon. "That."

I sit down next to her. The moon is the brightest I've ever seen it from right here. The trees are hands grasping for it, ready to scoop it up with long and gnarly fingers, just missing it, so it hangs there just out of reach.

"It's perfect."

"Yup," she says.

"What do you think happened to the train? How did that one car end up sitting by the river like that?"

"Laziness, probably," she says.

I baby-step my way across the ice until I'm next to her, then scoot down.

"Like it fell off and someone said screw it, just leave it there?"

"Something like that."

"I hope someone had something really amazing happen inside it and decided to put it there so they could always come to it. Maybe someone in love."

"Jesus, Lucille."

I hunch in on myself.

We sit a while, and the moon sings brightness to me until I relax again. All my inside chatter stops, and I am here — next to Eden, who knows me, who is maybe, miraculously, talking to me again.

"You know that Dylan Thomas poem?" Her hair drips down her back from underneath her little black hat.

I shrug.

"You remember, I know you do," she says. "Last year we had it in English." We always have that class together.

"Just the last two lines," I say. By the light of the moon her eyes are a wicked bright green. "'Do not go gentle into that good night. Rage, rage against the dying of the light.'"

She smirks, puts out her cigarette. "Well, color me shocked. You quoted."

"I did. You can color me shocked too."

"Do you get sick of me spouting quotes?"

"I missed them so much," I say.

The truth is, I forgot her wise words from other people, her easy way of being passionate and graceful. The peace I feel, the calm, when I'm with her. I forgot about how I need her. She knows life is a pillow that's all on my face, almost

almost suffocating me. But whoever is holding the pillow lets me breathe just enough so I don't die. I almost forgot that when I'm with Eden, she slaps away at the pillow and I can see something else.

Maybe everyone has a pillow like that.

Everything is more than one thing.

She pulls out a tiny bottle and hands it to me, rubs her gloved hands together.

"Tequila."

"Yeah?"

"Mom made tequila lime pie. Leftovers just sitting on the shelf. Seemed like a waste. Besides, it's ass cold out here."

It burns going down and I hate the way it tastes, but I drink it anyway. I get warm, warmer all over. Everything slows down and I settle back on the rock.

"So what's going on with you?" I ask.

Her eyes get huge and she clutches at her heart and looks at me like she's so surprised.

"Oh please," I say.

"It's been a while since you asked," she says.

"I've had a lot going on."

"Yeah." She takes another pull off the bottle. "I know. So much."

"No . . ." I falter. "Not that."

"I know," she says. "A lot of everything."

She reaches into her inside pocket and pulls out her pack of American Spirits. Yellow. It takes her a while to light her smoke, and her fingers shake some. She's chain-smoking.

"I went into the city the other day to take class with the Bolshoi," she says.

"Oh my gosh!" I picture her swooping across the stage and being flawless. "That's incredible!"

"I sucked," she says, and then something like a laugh comes out. It reminds me of Digby's not-laugh laugh.

"That's impossible," I say.

"No, Lu. It's not. It turns out that around here I'm pretty spectacular."

"You *are* spectacular —"

"For here, sure."

"Okay, so what?"

"So, there I'm not so awesome. There I'm barely average."

"But that doesn't make any sense. What you can do. How you bend."

"It's not good enough. Not by a lot. And according to the teacher there, if I'm not in the game now, I might as well forget about it. In ballet years, I'm practically middle-aged."

I look closer. She has bruisy crescents under her eyes and she is extra bony.

"I'm sorry, E." I put my arm around her shoulder while she takes more drags. It's an odd sensation to be the one doing the covering. "This is my fault. I distracted you."

"Stop trying to make everything about you, Lucille. This is about capacity."

I pause. "There has to be one of your quotes for this."

"If thou sucketh at balleteth, go ye into the darkness?"

"No." I squeeze. "Something else. It's in there."

I'm starting to feel woozy.

"Your turn," she says. "Tell me what's going on with you. Start with your mom. Anything?"

"Nothing from her." I take my arm away. "I saw my dad, though."

"Shut the front door!"

"Yesterday."

"And?"

"He's a douche too. Living in some halfway house,

avoiding reality, dreaming about beer. I got double douched in the parent department."

"He was the coolest."

I grab the tequila off the rock and polish it off in one swig.

"Sorry," she says. "What I mean is that, when we were little, he wasn't all uptight like the other dads."

"I guess. He's kind of cool in a non-dad way."

"I always thought he was kind of hot, actually."

"Oh, ewwwwwwwww."

"I mean, his hot value has definitely diminished since he did what he did, but I'm just saying. When we were little, I was jealous. Your dad played guitar —"

"Bass," I say.

"Okay, bass. And he skated. What other dad do you know who can do tricks on a skateboard?"

"It's the Cali in him. Or maybe the boy."

"Like I said, it was kind of hot."

Yuck. Enough of that.

"Yours seems pretty great," I say. "He does normal dad stuff. Plays ball, all that."

"Works all the time. Always has. Pokes his head out to make an I-don't-want-to-get-my-ass-left appearance. Leaves my mom to do everything around the house. She makes like she doesn't care, but I know she does. It has to smart. I think that's why she makes everything about us."

"At least he doesn't crumble at the first sign of stress."

"Yeah," she says. "But did you ever think about what it means to raise a family?"

"Like the pressure or something?"

"Did you ever think human beings aren't really cut out for it?"

"Maybe."

"'What man is such a coward he would rather not fall once than stand forever tottering?' Most people totter their whole lives. They never let themselves fall, never take the hit. They just go along, trying to do what they think they're supposed to. They never try to find out what's true for them, because that would mean being brave in a way people aren't."

"Do you think you are?"

"What?"

"A coward."

"Sometimes, I guess. I try not to be. What about you?"

I think about Digby. What we've been doing. How we've been doing it. Elaine. All those kisses swirl in me, and I'm honestly not sure whether everything I've done with Digby makes me brave or cowardly. Which is it when you're following your heart?

What I would say if I could: *Light, he's like the light. He put his hand on my arm and I can still feel it, Eden. We ate cheesesteaks. He remembered my favorite food. He played me music. He has the most perfect lips ever, like silk. He kisses me like home. When he helps me, it's the best help. When he's gone, I'm the most alone.*

I drop her finger. "I'm so fucked."

"Wow, Fred's has done wonders for your vocabulary, just as I predicted."

"I'm being serious. Don't make jokes." I dig out a little shard of ice from next to me, toss it into the river. "Isn't it crazy that with my whole life in pieces, it's your brother giving me the most trouble?"

She watches me for a long time. "He won't leave her easy, you know."

I nod.

"They have plans, a life they've been figuring out. They're going to school together next year if they both get in. They may have gotten a little ... disconnected ... but change costs him."

"Change costs everyone, Eden. And what if it's the truth

for him? What if *I'm* the truth for him? Would he really let that go out of fear, because he doesn't want to hurt anyone?"

"The devil you know, Lu. He needs to know what to expect."

"Because he's a coward?"

"Because he's good. A person like Digby needs a steady thing."

And I am not steady.

I snort, because if I don't, I'll just start crying.

"Really," she says. "The world is a little much for him. The way people are. He's all ripped up that he's doing this to her. Doesn't know which way is up. He's just spinning and spinning in circles. And he loves her, you know? A lot."

"He talks to you about it?"

"Why do you think I've been staying away from you?"

"Because you were mad?"

"Oh, Lulu. No. Not really. That night you got the bloody nose, when you went all psycho, I saw how he was looking at you, how he was so ready to compromise everything for you. I love you so much, and I wasn't even ready to do that. I don't want to be caught between the two of you. This is a mess, and he's my twin. The only person who comes before you.

Once I saw that he was crazy about you, I had to pick." She kicks at her rock with her ankle boots. "He's so confused. I've never seen him like this before. Don't break him, Lu," she says. "This thing that's between you? It's messing him up. He's hobbled by his own good heart."

I nod again, feel like the ground is getting so far away, think about Dad, about how he broke. Maybe we're all breakable. It's just a question of what breaks us.

"You love him?" she asks. "Really?"

I don't see the point in denying it. "Completely."

"Then the best thing you can do for him is let him go. You're already stuck somewhere too messy to recover from."

"He said that?"

"I'm saying that."

"And they'll just go on like normal?"

She shrugs. "You'll find someone else, you know. I heard somewhere that there are ten thousand people on earth that each of us can be compatible with. He's not the only one."

Everything in me wants to protest. I don't want to find another person. I want Digby. And she knows, she knows there's only one of him.

"You've got enough to deal with without him," she says. "Right now, you have to rage."

I've got nothing without him. Nothing. Nothing but rage. But I'm tired of being a human respirator, of Digby being my only oxygen. It can't be good. Not for anyone.

She pulls her phone out of her leather and looks at the time. "Damn."

"Eden," I say.

"Yeah?"

"I'm really sorry about the ballet thing. You should keep on."

"Oh, I will. Just now I know it's not going to do me any good." She squints at me. "And don't try to tell me any different. Denial is for losers. Face your crap and move on. Otherwise you'll get old and depressed and turn into a scary pod person whose most pressing issue in life is when they get to trade in the can of Dr Pepper for the can of Bud."

I laugh.

"It's true," she says. "Look around." She smashes out her cigarette and leaves it on the rock.

I pick it up, and as I do she stretches up tall, puts her hands above her head like she's about to do a pirouette, and her heel slips on a little bit of ice right next to our rock. How her foot is in just the wrong place, and how she loses her footing and wobbles.

Tottering now.

She doesn't recover. She keeps falling. There's no tread on her shoes and both legs are out from under her and *thunk* and Eden hits her head hard on the pointy part of our rock.

Quick stand to catch her. She's already down. *Reach for me,* I say with my hand. She doesn't. She's limp. Slides down a slick sheet of ice. I am colder and hotter. I reach for her, and she is already gone all the way away from me.

Everything is quiet but the rushing water, whose currents are more powerful than the cold.

Eden is in the water before I know what's happening, and her eyes are closed and her hair is floating all around her.

Ophelia.

I am running. I don't slip on the ice. Not once, not even a little. Splashing down into the water, and it is like a knife that stabs me everywhere at once, ten katrillion needles slicing through my skin. I have to get out of this water. I have to get farther in, get to her. I kick off my boots under the water. She is already far away, floating silent. I scream and I scream again and it just goes into nothing.

My scream gets sucked up by the night's black.

I want my sword and my shield, and I want to save

Eden because she is love for me now, but I don't have those things, and how would they help me fight water? I could see everything before and now I can't see Eden at all. She's going around the bend and I. Will. Catch. Her. Then the river runs through me, pushes me to her. I might drown and I am all Wren has and I can't see Eden anymore and then I have her. I have Eden by the collar on her leather jacket. I scream and hold on to her and nobody can hear me and my throat hurts. I drag and I drag, river fighting me now, and I pull until I am at rocks. Slip. Ice. Rock. Grab. Got. I have a rock and I pull so hard and my body is numb and Wren is home alone and I yank. Get her out. No breath.

My phone.

Where is it?

I can't call the police, the ambulance.

I am doing everything.

Everything wrong.

I am shaking, shaking, and I unzip her jacket, wrench Digby's keys out of her inside pocket, try to pull her with me and there's no way. I climb the bank and run, now slipping on ice with no shoes, until I hit the path out to the street, my body burning cold. It is so familiar. I know every step, every car parked on the road. I run to the Beast, but my hands are shaking too hard, I would never make it to the police station. Too far. Which house to go to?

Eden alone. Wren alone. Me alone.

Digby.

This door. This door belongs to the lady who gardens all day in the summer in a big pink hat. I bang with my whole body. I bang my fist under the sign that says IF THE HOUSE BURNS DOWN, PLEASE SAVE THE CAT. It shows a cat reading a book, and that makes me shake harder. The door takes a million years to open.

The lady answers, and she is wearing a pink robe the same color as her hat and she says oh my god as she opens the door and I am shaking and I put my wet hands on her and my body falls into her softness and I shudder call, call, call 911. Please. My friend, my best friend is dying. My best friend hit her head on a rock and she is dying.

Please, I am screaming with everything I have into her pink face, and the shoulder of her pink robe, so she will hear me, so someone will finally hear. Call.

Day 1

Coca-Cola went to town
Diet Pepsi shot him down

I squeeze Wren.

The respirator machine pumping air into Eden's lungs goes *shakaaaawah, shakaaaawah, shakawaaaah,* and her head is covered in white gauze. They drilled holes in her skull to relieve the pressure from the swelling, but she didn't wake up. She's in a coma, no permanent brain damage according to what they gathered from the scans, and now we wait.

Janie brought me clothes and shoes after she took Digby to pick up his truck, so I am Eden head to toe.

Digby wraps an arm around me, all the trouble between us tossed to the side. We're there at the bedside, Digby, Wren, and me. Janie and John are somewhere talking to people about important things. Thoughts are hard to catch. Everything drifts. My whole chest is an ache. Flowers are starting to come in, adding color and taking away space.

"Why don't you go and have some food at the house?" Janie says when she gets back.

John has his arm around her waist. I don't think I've ever seen them that way, hugged together.

"Don't worry, Janie, she'll wake up," Wren says, watching Eden, who looks so, so small under a pink blanket. She would hate that blanket. I hate that blanket. I don't think I will ever like pink again. "She's strong."

"Yes, honey, she is strong," Janie says, "but even so . . ."

"No," Wren says. "Not like regular people. She's super-strong."

Janie starts to cry.

After I get some weekend girl named Delaney to cover my shift at Fred's, we go to Eden's house for dinner, like Janie said. She steers me into the Beast with Digby. The gearshift goes up to first. Down to second. Up to third. We rumble into Digby's driveway, John right behind us in his shiny black truck. How has a day passed, when the last one never went anywhere? How am I still awake? I'm so tired, I can barely feel my feet, and I want to go lie down on Eden's bed and shove my face into her blankets. I want to pull Digby into a corner with me and kiss him so I know I'm still here. All of that wanting is as wrong as everything else, so I sit at the dinner table instead.

Eden's house is all full of casseroles and pies, and it's only been a few hours. *Heat at 350° for 45 minutes,* says the crumpled note in the middle of the table. The curly writing was carefully done, like someone took care with those few words. Like they thought, maybe my old family recipe for lasagna can take a little bite out of your pain.

I keep waiting for someone to yell at me, but no one does. They should, though. No one eats except Wren, who is in front of the TV, watching *Adventure Time.* Gooey, cheesy lasagna coagulates around mushrooms and ground beef in the middle of the table and on all of our plates, and we all just sit there. Me, Digby, and John. There are too many empty chairs. The table is too big. BC is turning circles around himself like he has no place to be. No one is talking. You could hear chewing if anyone were eating. It's so quiet except for Wren's cartoon, and even that is absorbed into the furniture, the way my screaming got sucked into the water.

And then the person with the pillow is pushing all the way down with big, evil hands. Huge sounds are about to come out of me. It can't happen now, not when these people are waiting and waiting. The chair jerks when I slide up.

I barely make it down the hall to the bathroom before it comes, wheezing like my lungs are trying to climb out of my body. The whole thing is too loud, and I flip on the switch that runs the fan, and turn on the water. I even flush the toilet, and all the while I am holding on to the side of the sink, waiting for it to stop, but it doesn't. It just keeps coming, but there are no tears and everything gets very far away and prickly. And then I am throwing up all the nothing inside my stomach. I taste tequila and the smoke from Eden's cigarette, like time in reverse, and then it's just bile, just trickles of more nothing. I wipe my mouth and stand up straight.

I see it all. The softest lavender towels, the striped lavender and cream wallpaper, the special sink that looks like it's a floating crystal bowl, the white ceramic soap dispenser. The matching toothbrush holder with the two toothbrushes inside. A razor that must be Digby's, and shaving gel that's wintery fresh and guarantees smoothness and no bumps! The wooden heart jewelry box that has Eden's favorite things inside. The container that holds Eden's headband for washing her face, and her soap. Everything in here is soft and warm and clean.

And Eden's earrings are sitting by the side of the sink on the floating crystal shelf. They're the little silver dangly ones that she got on vacation in New Mexico last year. She wears them all the time. They were just in her ears, hooked through her skin. Maybe she even took them off right before she texted me so she could just come home and get right into bed.

I run my fingers across the pounded metal. It's warm.

I wish I couldn't see so clearly.

I wipe under my eyes and blow my nose, make my breaths come out even for real. I'm in sweatpants and a hoodie and I'm still cold, like the river has followed me in here and is still digging into my skin, like it's never going to let me go. Will I ever be warm again?

Eden has to wake up.

I don't want to scare Wren when I go back out, even though she's seen all of us lose it by now, so I splash some water on my face and wipe it down with one of the softie towels, and I take some more good, long, deep breaths and throw my shoulders back, and then I am ready.

I open the door as quietly as I can, and Digby is leaning

against the other side of the wall in the hallway. His face is a little gaunt, all pale, and with my clear vision I see his eyes are that color that you see sometimes in advertisements for trips to faraway island places, and he has those freckles like someone put them there, one by one, so carefully. Like someone took a paintbrush and said, *that one will look just perfect right there, and that one right there.* And there's the angle, the shape of him against the wall. His torso takes up so much room, and he's thin but not. And his clothes, the way they hang off of him, it's like there's room for someone to fit there, like there's too much room, and like they're comfortable, like being in them or next to them would be so good. His eyes are big right now, so open, and they aren't asking me any questions, not even telling me anything. They are just looking at me like they see everything.

"I'm sorry," I say.

"Why are you sorry?" he says, and his voice is deep and rubs up against itself. "You saved her."

"I was the reason she was there. I should have known better, with the ice and everything."

He kicks at my shin. "Stop. *You* didn't slip. Shit happens."

"Yeah," I say, "it sure does. But I'm sorry I let her fall."

His shoulders start to shake. He stays against the wall, but he opens his arms and there is his black hoodie like the one Eden always wears, like the one I'm wearing. And then I am pressed against it, my face in his chest, his arms around me. And then he is a pillow, but a different kind, one to fall into. One that catches and holds and doesn't smother at all, except I know he is falling right now too. I push him into the wall like I want him to go through it, and his arms get tighter and I want them tighter still.

I thought I would be able to keep it together, but something about him, about being cocooned by him like this—surrounded in black with the pressure of his arms against my back—it makes everything come out.

His heart beats against me like it's fighting for breath, like it's gone feral and wants to escape. I want to climb inside his chest and hold it in my hands. I want to stay here forever.

I touch his cheek. I run my hand all the way down his arm. His face is wet, and I take the sleeve of my sweatshirt and pull it down over my other hand, and I reach up and wipe it like I would do for Wren. He holds my wrist, keeps me from touching him anymore.

"She was there and talking to me, and then she was still," I say, and slide down the wall. He slides down next to me. "It was so fast."

"I thought I could be like Joan of Arc," I say.

"You are Joan of Arc. You got her out."

"Maybe not fast enough."

"It was the hit she took to the back of the head. She'd be dead if you hadn't jumped in after her."

I nudge him and he nudges me back. We both know she would be in the living room right now if I hadn't texted her in the first place, but his kindness makes a difference anyway.

The doorbell ding-dongs down the hall, and John answers.

A sweet and clipped voice says, *I'm so sorry I didn't get here sooner. I was out of range and I just got the news.*

Digby stands.

Elaine.

So Many Years Ago

When we moved in, I knew there were kids next door. I heard them stomping up and down the stairs, arguing with their parents, laughing all the time. I smelled food cooking, things like bacon and maybe pie. If I stood in just the right place, I could hear the water running for their baths and showers, could hear them brushing their teeth. I prowled the house those first days, learning Digby and Eden, though I didn't know it was them. It took me a while before I dared to venture outside the house. The air felt thick and foreign compared with the easy California feel I was used to. I was helium.

It's his hair I remember first, the day I finally went

outside. That color, like a little piece of sunset got dropped on his head. And the boys crashing into each other as they played ball across the street. Something swished around in me.

Digby was gentle, playing with the friends who are still his friends. He didn't push or call names like the other boys. He just ran, dodged, and weaved like he was doing exactly the right thing, like he was some kind of tree, long and graceful.

That's when the voice came from the adjoining porch. "Do you live here now?" it said.

I nodded at the girl.

"Before, there was a lady," she said. "She's dead."

"My aunt."

The girl seemed to consider this information, then dismiss it as irrelevant.

"There's only boys on this block." The noodly girl nodded across the street. "That's my brother, Digby." She showed me her uneven half-baby, half-grown teeth. Such a good smile. "And my name is Eden."

Day 2

school.

It's not the flowers that get me, or even the candles. It's how many there are. You would think Eden was dead. People amaze me, how they need to jump on every tragedy or even potential tragedy like it belongs to them, how they can't leave well enough alone when they get the chance to be involved in something. Facebook and all that makes it even worse. Even though my phone was stupid and didn't have the Internet anyway, I'm almost glad it's gone now, even though it means if Mom were to try . . .

Who am I kidding? She's not going to try.

Cards and pictures and graffiti on Eden's locker, on the wall next to it. Who did all this? What time did they get here? I want to read everything they say, but I don't because I feel like everyone is looking at me, and that makes me realize how much I slip through everything, unseen, how much I like that no one sees me, or that they try not to. It's like the opposite of when Dad flipped out in the street. He gifted me my repellent quality. No one wants anything to do with the crazy guy's daughter.

Now, give them a coma and all bets are off. That's like throwing pieces of flesh at hungry sharks. I am half expecting everyone standing around the spectacle to break into some variation of "Kumbaya," and I'm thinking that might make me a little nuts. I am thinking I'm already a little nuts.

Touched, Mom used to say.

Untouched. Too much touched. Sometimes it's hard to say.

Sometimes you just have to walk away, which is what I do now.

On my way down the hall, I squeeze past the growing crowd like a freak fish flopping against the current, trying not to have overly hostile thoughts about fake friends. Elaine is coming toward me, and when we make eye contact I am caught. Turn back and face the insanity, or talk to her. There's nowhere to go.

"Do you believe this?" Elaine says.

"Feeding frenzy," I say.

"People will be people, I guess." I search for signs that Elaine knows anything, and I find this instead: nice, conversational, distant, concerned maybe. Then, "Are you going to the hospital?"

"I have some things to take care of this afternoon, but I'm going to try to go after school." I hesitate. "You?"

"Not today. But I'll be there tomorrow."

Perfect face. Oval, zero pores on her creamy olive skin, full lips, high cheekbones, eyes to dive into and I'm-a-smart-person glasses, cute little button nose, shiny straight black hair. Her clothes look new, clean and ironed. She is bright and clear.

I float, then, away from all of this, until she brings me back.

"Lucille?"

"Yeah?" I say. "I have to go to class."

She puts a hand on my arm. Stops me.

"It's really crazy what you did. Jumping in the river like that." She's touching me, and I want to tell her everything, confess and hope she will absolve me.

"Anyone would," I say.

"I don't know." She squeezes. "I don't know about that. Anyway, you got her out. Not everyone would have done that."

I say something, I'm not sure what, and walk away, nodding and bobbling, because she can't do that. It's not allowed.

Don't be nice to me, Elaine. Please don't do that.

I am at the hospital again. The goddess nurse named Rita glides in and out of the room and sashays around me, tutting and humming. Wren sleeps in the chair. My elbows have sunk into the putrid pink. Janie has gone home for an hour, just to shower and eat something. Digby isn't anywhere.

Eden is skeletal. I should talk to her. That's what you're supposed to do, anyway.

The machine goes *shakaaaawah, shakaaaawah, shaka-waaaah.*

The other machine goes *beep, beep, beep.*

My head collapses between my arms.

I am literally unable to take normal breaths, and I'm shaking all over when I walk into Fred's with Wren. I go in through the back door, past the cooks, and Fred is nowhere in sight. The dishwasher waves and says hi in Spanish.

"Hola," I say, digging past my fear and relief at seeing and then not seeing Fred around every corner. Then I scoot past the walk-in, where he's hunched over a container of green chile, moving it somewhere, and everything speeds up.

The dining room is pretty much set, and the girls are milling about. The crosses all over the walls. I don't know that I've ever paid attention to them until now. They are everywhere, every version, every possible configuration of a crucifix. My mind wants to get to the bottom of why that matters.

I don't know if I still have a job, I don't know how pissed off Fred is about finding me making out by the bathrooms when I was supposed to be working. No matter what's going on with Eden, I can't afford to lose my job.

Fortunately, Wren has no idea about any of it, really, and I figure she acts as some kind of barrier between me and the potential forty lashes that are coming my way. At first when I step through the back door, no one pays attention. Shane and Rachel are sitting at table six, reading something. I try to be quiet, but Wren says, "Hi, guys!" and they look up and then they are on me, around me giving me hugs, hugging Wren, too.

"Girl," Shane says to me, "how did you not tell us that you got into all this?"

She holds up the *Cherryville Squire,* and there in that crappy small-town paper is a picture of Eden, a story about us. The headline reads LOCAL STAR BALLERINA IN COMA. I can't see any more than that, what with Shane shaking the thing, but there's a picture of Eden, one of me, too, my school picture from last year. I look so clean on the black-and-white, almost pretty, almost normal.

Rachel ticks at Wren's chin, tells her, "Your sister did something really special."

"We were just at the hospital," Wren says, and she goes into the back, to play with the makeup, I'm sure.

"Yeah," I say, "ask Eden how I did."

214

"It doesn't matter," Rachel says. "That's not what matters, sweetie." She goes off after Wren.

"Thanks," I mumble at her back.

"You're here?" Val comes up behind us looking especially vampy. There is latex involved in her outfit, and her eyeliner is extra thick. "Shouldn't you be somewhere else?"

"I need to work," I say.

"Right," Shane says. "Life keeps on." Her phone buzzes on the table and she picks it up, grunts. "Hm. Wouldn't you know? Trent. They need to be blown off at least once a month, just so they remember."

"You need to talk to Fred," Val says.

"Yeah," Shane says. "Like, now."

"What are you doing here?" The voice behind me is flat, devoid of anything identifiable.

Fred.

I am so fired.

The dining room clears out so fast, you'd think someone had let off tear gas in the place, and then it's just me and Fred. He sits down, and the paper with my picture is next to his wrist.

He tells me to sit, and then it's like I'm in *The Godfather*. I'd like to stuff some cotton balls into Fred's cheeks so we could go all the way with this, but I don't think he'd take kindly. I don't think he's in the mood for me at all.

My legs feel weak, my head is starting to ache, and something burns in my throat.

"So you're back." He seems wan, like the zombie apocalypse he's always waiting for came and got him.

I say, "I covered my shift."

"Yeah, but"—he clicks at the paper with his fingernail—"you got a lot going on."

I'm pretty sure my lymph nodes just got bigger.

"So what is it?" he says.

"Can I work?"

"Your sister here again?"

The tablecloth under the plastic has flags on it.

"I saw her in the back," he says. "You gonna keep her here all night?"

I scoot back in my chair. "Okay, so I'm fired, right?"

He stands up and paces for a second. I want to bolt. I don't need to sit around for this. And he looks mad. Supermad.

"You're makin' out with people in the halls. You bail before you're done with your side work. You bring your kid sister to work with you." He scoots his glasses back on his nose, reaches inside his pocket for a cigarette, lets it hang between his fingers. "What am I supposed to do?"

"I get it, okay?"

"No, it's not okay. You are part of a team. You have to act like it."

I don't know what that means, and that's fine because he's not done talking. I sit here like I'm five and take my medicine.

"You're jumping into rivers and shit, and you don't even tell me. Best friend's in a coma? And who's that guy with his hands all over you, anyway? And why do you have your sister with you?" He puts his hands on the table. "Where are your parents, Lucille?"

I'm out of here. I'm out. I am almost by him, but he grabs my arm. "Uh-uh," he says. "Think I don't know about your dad?"

"I'm sure you do," I push past my swollen throat. "Everybody knows about that."

"That's right. And I know your mom's not around either. I don't know why, but I know that. I know you need this job, so why don't you trust me and act like you need this as much as you do."

"Why?" I ask. "What for?"

"So we can help you."

His eyes are really blue. I've never had him this close to me before. His breath is all coffee and cigarettes, but his eyes are a blue that breaks right past his dirty lenses.

"I never had a kid, Lucille, and I probably never will, unless I knock up some resistance hottie after the zombies come."

I smile.

I smiled!

"But if I had a kid, I would want one like you. One who doesn't sit around and wait for things to happen. I would want a badass chick for a daughter who goes out and gets a job and takes care of her own like you do that sister of yours. I would want one who jumps into rivers in the middle of the ever-loving night and pulls her best friend out of the water and saves her."

I start to say something, but he puts up his hand.

"I want you by my side when the zombies attack, okay?" He makes a weird digging motion with his hands. "I wouldn't say that to just anyone. Own that shit."

"So I'm not fired?"

"On one condition," he says. "We're going to sit down,

and you're going to tell me exactly what's going on with you. And you can't keep the kid here anymore. We'll figure something out. Get the girls to help out. Rachel can do her makeup on her nights off or something. And I swear to Christ if I catch that boy with his hands on you again, he's gonna meet my leetle friend." His hand is an unlit cigarette gun. "Together we stand, divided we fall."

He hoots, and it is so dumb that it kills the cry that wants to come.

He is such a cheeseball.

And so magnificent.

"Hey," he yells in the general direction of the office. "What's all the dilly-dallying for? Get your asses out here and start working! You got twenty minutes to get this goddamn place shipshape!"

Everyone shuffles out of the office and starts doing stuff.

His clammy hand is on my shoulder, then it reaches into his back pocket and pulls out some money. Four hundred dollars. "I already covered your shift today. You're going to take this and not say one single word. You take the week off, and I'll see you on Monday."

"Freddie . . ."

He cuts me off. "Not a word." He heads for the side door, surveys the room. "Well, okay then," he says. "Good."

When we get home, our house is spotless. I mean completely. Everything is suddenly at right angles. The cupboards are stocked too. I can't even get mad or scared or anything, even though I know I locked up before I took Wren to school this morning.

I have nothing left inside, no room for panic. Neither does Wren. We just look at each other when I get Wren her snack, and we have so much to choose from. We both head up to the bathroom so I can take my shower, and up there, too. New bottles of shampoo and conditioner, brand-new soap, a few new towels. Whoever this person is has gone to new and greater lengths. Or maybe it isn't a person at all. Maybe it really is magic. Maybe it is like Wren says. Maybe it's an angel with giant luminous wings, shopping at the Super Fresh in gauzy duds, clipping coupons and stuff.

Maybe I'm finally losing it for real.

Whatever.

This has been the longest day.

⚡

Eden once told me she wanted to be cremated. Said she didn't want worms in her. She wanted to be in one of those biodegradable urns that you plant somewhere with a seed in it so you become a tree. I thought it was romantic, cool. I figured a thousand years from now I would tell Eden's husband or kids what she wanted, that maybe we would get to be part of the same garden.

I wasn't thinking about Eden dying now, in reality.

Potential hypothetical death is way less scary than actual maybe really soon death.

What will I do without her if she doesn't survive? Life without my father I can take. My mother, even. And Digby. Thinking his name is too much for me. But I cannot withstand any more loss. I know in my bones that I can't.

Shakaaaawah.

"Wake up," I say to my best friend on this earth. "You hear me? You. Wake. Up."

Shakaaaawah. Beep. Beep. Beep.

"Please," I say. "Please."

Moving Day BD
(Before Digby)

"Why is it so hot?" Eden was laid out on her lounge chair, book over her face while I people watched and tried not to be too depressed. Mom and Wren were at the store, and Dad was still sleeping. There was a lot of foot traffic that day, car traffic too, what with the giant U-Haul pretty much blocking the street.

"Um, because it's July, and it's hot in July," I said.

"It's like God has a personal vendetta against the East Coast and has unleashed his wrath upon us with explosive heat and humidity." She perked up for a minute. "The new house has air conditioning. Like, real, actual air conditioning."

"How nice for you," I said.

John and Digby came out the door, each on one end of a desk, and shuffled to the truck.

"Are you serious right now?" Digby shot as he went.

"What?" Eden said. "All my stuff is packed."

"Yeah, but Mom's in there cleaning. You could help."

"I will, okay? I am taking a break." Eden flopped back down, wiped her forehead. "Pain in my ass."

"I'm going to miss you," I said. "Nothing is going to be right, now."

"Everything is going to be right," she said, stretching forward over one leg, tugging on the bottom of her foot. "It's just going to be different. Nothing wrong with different."

"Well, I like things the way they are."

She shrugged and pulled on her foot again.

"I guess if I was going to air conditioning and a custom-decorated house, I'd be okay with it too," I allowed. "But it's going to be boring and stupid without you."

"We'll meet," she said, proffering a pinky. "We'll meet at our spot anytime you want, whenever we feel like it."

I sat on the railing, tangled my pinky in hers.

"Promise?" I said.

"Oh, I promise." She leaned forward. "And, Lu, trust me when I say, whatever else, it will never be boring."

"What? The neighborhood? Yes it will. It will suck forever."

"No," she said, smirking as John and Digby came back toward the house. "Not the neighborhood, silly. I'm talking about life."

Day 3

(Wee Hours of Early Morning)

I come to consciousness back to front in pitch-black. I'm burning. That's the first thing I feel. I'm burning, not my skin so much, but my insides, all the way down. It's an ache that starts from somewhere I can't name, and I'm separating from my body it hurts so much. I would do anything to escape it.

Ashes to ashes to ashes to ashes.

I'm coming apart.

I have been dreaming something and the dream has chased me out.

It takes a long time. Hours to turn a body to ash, to basic chemical compounds for alternate disposal, to burn a person back into dust. You don't get incinerated in seconds or minutes. Even then there are teeth, bone fragments. I think that's how they do it. At night. They fire up the oven and cook you down, come back in the morning and fit you into one of those little boxes.

Eden's legs are so long. I don't want that to happen to her. Not now. Skin melted, muscles chewed away, and finally even the bones of her giving in and crumbling. No more arabesques. No more pliés. No more worrying about pointe, about whether she can make it, about anything. No worries. None of anything else, either.

Hot skin presses against my own. Eden with her flesh falling away and her eyes bulging. Feel her all on top of me in the dark. It's not Eden. Eden's not dead; she's at the hospital. My head isn't right.

It's Wren on me.

I lay a hand across her forehead, and my palm stings. I try to sit up, but I'm dizzy.

"Wrenny girl," I whisper, grasp around for the bedside lamp.

She moans. She is so hot.

I scramble. I have to.

⚡

I have no phone. I have no Tylenol. I don't know what to do, but we are both sick and something bad is going to happen to Wren if I don't take action. She doesn't argue or anything when I throw one of Mom's jackets over her.

She runs a hand over my face, says, "Oh, you're hot."

I grab a towel and get it wet. "Put this on you," I tell her. She holds it on her forehead, and I get her out into the cold. There's more snow on the ground, but it's not anything I can't handle. I get her in the car and drive.

Not to the hospital. I don't want to go there. I go up.

To the cul-de-sac.

I knock at the door a lot before I remember the doorbell, and then I push that. It's white and shiny under the street-lamp and I'm not hot anymore. I'm the coldest I've ever been.

I never saw Janie look like that before, little pieces of her red hair like an electrocuted Raggedy Ann. When she saw Wren, she uncrossed her arms and took us in, cooing. She's spending her first night home away from the hospital. John is there instead. And we had to get sick now and keep her from sleeping.

Tut-tut, she says. She's not sleeping anyway.

I know this room so well. Eden's. The softest down blankets and pillows, all that certain cream color, the hardwood floors, the plush rectangular matchy carpet. The prints of ballerinas on the walls, mostly black-and-whites, framed. The books and books and books, so many, all worn along their spines, and the shelf. Every pair of Eden's ballet shoes from tiny all the way up. The closet, half open, all the clothes swishing and shimmering in there. If I open the drawers, I will find all the leotards, the leg warmers. The bulk of Eden. And then up on the ceiling above my head, that newest and best quote. The last quote, maybe. DO NOT GO GENTLE INTO THAT GOOD NIGHT. RAGE, RAGE AGAINST THE DYING OF THE LIGHT. Again.

Janie has Wren in the living room so she can keep an extra-close eye on her. It's hollow without her on me, but I can also just lie here, full of antifever medication, tea at the bedside, and do nothing.

Thoughts get watery. There was something sleepy in the meds.

Is Eden in her body? Does she know her dad is next to her? Does she know I'm sorry? Will she dance again or will she burn? Where's Mom?

Maybe Eden is going to flit through the door any second

and bounce onto the bed. She will tuck her chin into her hands, hair falling all around her heart face, and she will say, "Tell me, li'l Lulu. Tell me everything."

How Digby ends up in bed with me, I don't really know.

I'm sweating. Because my fever broke or because of this. Breathing makes time go faster, and I don't want time to do anything at all. I want time to take a vacation. I want to give it a pink slip, walking papers. *Beat it, time.* This is where I want to be forever. With Digby.

I am also not breathing because of Digby's hand. It has crept under the blankets and is on my waist now. Moving. Just a little bit, not too much, but it is. An inch up. An inch down. So soft, like it's daring, but only just. If he stops, I will spontaneously combust. It's vicious how much I want to move into him, but I make myself stay still, just shaking on the inside, maybe on the outside some too. I don't know.

He trembles like me. I can hear it, the way his breath is coming out. But his hand is sure. That part of him dips under my T-shirt and rolls over the skin underneath. I wish it was everywhere. I want to turn over. I don't want to do anything that will make the lights come on, that will make this stop, and Elaine is in my head somewhere, though I try to push her out because she doesn't belong here. This is between Digby and me.

Just us.

Which is when we hear Janie. Sobbing. It isn't a human sound. It's like a wolf, like a ghost, muffled in something, but not enough. Not with the house so quiet.

Digby's hand goes still.

"Closet," he whispers into my neck. "She's been crying in her closet."

A mother's cry curdles cream and skin pulls tighter and Digby and I wrench our bodies against it, squeeze even closer together.

It's like Janie is begging.

still Day 3

I wake up like someone shook me.
It's Eden-blanket pink outside. Digby's legs are over mine,
one arm slung across my back.

Things are a little blurry. Then I see.

Eden is in the room with us. Sitting on the bed at our
feet, perched like she would be, chin on knees. Her head is
cocked to the side. Watching. And she is smiling.

I close my eyes again, Digby's mouth on my neck.

"I'm going back to the hospital," Janie says. She towers over
Digby and me, fully dressed, hair pinned back, no more

strays. She is holding a glass of water out to me, and a couple of white pills.

I am awake too fast, dizzy again. I smooth myself down, pull at my—Eden's—shirt. My throat hurts awful.

"Digby, there's a two-hour delay today again because of the snow, and I don't want anyone going anywhere until I get back. I have to go relieve John at the hospital, but there's plenty of food in the fridge and I've given Wren another dose of medication. Here's yours." She thrusts the pills at me.

"Mom—" Digby tries.

"No," she says. "I don't want to hear it right now. Later."

Eden. My dream.

"Is Eden okay?" I ask.

"She's in a coma, Lucille," she says. "No. She is not okay." She flails her arms around. "None of this is okay."

"Oh," I say.

"You two had better start thinking about what is going on here. In the midst of a family crisis, Digby Riley Jones? Really? This cannot go on. As far as I can tell, everything has gone to hell in a handbasket." When I've taken the pills, she puts a hand out for the water and I give it back to her. "How does your mother leave you like that? I mean, I have a child in the hospital and she doesn't even have the decency to take care of her own children. It's unbelievable, just unbelievable. And now the two of you. I don't have time for this!" Her voice is so close to hysterical that I only briefly stop to wonder how long she's known about Mom and how much she knows. "I have had enough." Her voice breaks on the last word, and she walks out, just like that, half slams the door on her way.

"Damn," Digby says. "Dammit."

He plays basketball. Really. Once the pills kick in and I feel half normal again and my throat stops hurting so much, I look outside because I can't find him anywhere. He has cleared off just that one patch of the driveway and he is throwing the ball in the hoop. Black beanie on, sporty jacket and pants, tossing the ball over and over. Bounce, bounce. Through the window, his face scrunches like he's looking for something in that hoop, all surrounded by white. Black and white.

"Can I have some water?" Wren says. "And can you put on the Food Network?"

"Sure." I feel awful and she looks a little worse than me, but I'm walking and not so delirious anymore. I hope I didn't infect Digby. After I get her all set up, I go outside with my jacket on over my sleeping clothes.

"Hey," I say.

Digby stops for a second, then keeps going. Bouncing and running. He swishes by me, the sound of his pants rubbing together. The cold day is a relief.

"You should go back inside," he says finally, dribbling the ball.

"I'm not going to, though," I say.

He plays like I'm not there, and then he smashes the ball hard against the wall, close enough to me that I start. It bounces into the road. We both watch it until it rolls under Mom's car and into a tire.

"Did you know green eyes and red hair are the rarest combination of traits?" I say.

"Yeah," he says. "You're pretty much the queen of non sequiturs, you know that?"

He comes a little closer.

"You're rare is what I mean," I say.

"You are too."

"Maybe," I say. Then, "Digby, do you want to be with me?"

He dribbles the ball, not looking at me.

"Do you?" I say. "Because you can't have both. You can't have everything the way it was at the same time as you make something new. You can't," I struggle, "touch me like that and then disappear. And if you can't stand by me, hold my hand, be proud to be with me, then you can't have the rest. It's not fair to anyone, not even you. So what do you want?"

He doesn't answer, just breathes fog in and out. The crack inside me turns to a fissure turns to a split. I will not think about his hands on me. It's done.

"I'm going home," I say. "I know your mom is upset, but tell her we'll be okay. I'll get some medicine on my way." I wrap myself tighter.

"The whole thing—"

"The whole thing is messed up. Messy. Unfixable."

"It is?"

"Of course it is." I breathe on my icy hand, think about what Eden said. "I have a lot of things I have to figure out right now, and I can't do it here. You have a lot too. Thanks for everything, okay? For helping with Wren and being there. You were beyond. But now you have to stay away. Say goodbye to me."

"Come on, Lucille."

"Say it."

"You're being so . . ."

"I know, dramatic. This is high drama. But you have to say it anyway." I'm nodding because with every second I'm surer that I'm doing something good, something necessary for everyone. "Because next time you see me, we have to be like we were before. There has to be an end. You see that, right?"

My teeth start to chatter and he goes to put an arm around me, but I move away.

"Nothing ever ends," he says.

"Not true," I say. "Everything does."

"But what if it's you?" He pulls at his head. "What if I do the wrong thing?"

"Cut it out." I want to say bitter things I can't take back, like to man up, but I force myself to my original thought. I love him too much. That's what's under everything. He makes me weak. I don't like weak. Eden said he is good. I want to be uncomplicated. Good, too. I want to be normal, clean, with two nice parents and a sweet boyfriend who doesn't have to sneak. "I'm not going to the hospital today since I'm sick," I say, "but if I'm better, I'd like to go tomorrow after school. If that's okay."

"So you don't want me to be there?" He looks small.

"I think it's better if you're not, but I will stay away if that's when you want to go."

"It's down to this." Shakes his head. "Unbelievable."

"For a little while." I pat him on his arm. "We'll be friends again someday, when all of this fades. Tell your mom thanks for last night." I nod toward my car. "Better get your ball before I run it over. I'm going to get Wren."

I look back one time before I go in the house. I'm hoping whatever he's doing, I can freeze it in my head so I'll always remember it. I know I'll see Digby again—a million times, probably—but it won't be like this. He's leaning against the post for the basketball hoop, doubled over, staring at his feet.

"Bye, Lucille Bennett," he says as I close the door.

A *ratatatatat* sound wakes me up, climbs the stairs, and breaks through my NyQuil fuzz. Wren doesn't budge next to me. I'm so disoriented, I have to hold on to the wall on my way down. I don't have much time to think about who it might be. Dad? No. Mom? No. Maybe Digby or Janie?

Seriously, in all my wildest imaginings, Elaine is the

very, very last person I expect when I open the door. But there she is. Her little olive face is wrecked, puffy and . . .

"What time is it?" I say.

She swipes at her eyes. "Were you asleep?"

"I'm sick."

She steps back a little, stands up straighter.

"At least he wasn't lying about something," she mutters.

And then I know. It comes into focus. "Do you want to come in?" I say.

"No!" She folds her arms over her navy blue cashmere sweater. "Maybe." She looks around. "It's cold."

She glances around. I am not going to think about what her privileged eyes are seeing. I'm just not. "It's only nine o'clock. I'm sorry if I woke you."

"You're apologizing to me?"

"Right? Right." She reaches into her purse for a tissue.

And then she's in my house.

"I want to yell at you," she says in a shaky voice.

"Go ahead," I say. "You can yell at me if you want to."

The tears spill over her bottom lids then and rush down her cheeks.

My head and chest pound.

"Are you sleeping with him?"

"No," I say. *Worse,* I think.

She paces around a second, touches the wall, the molding, then meets my eyes. There's something tough in there.

"Well, that's good I guess." She faces me like a mirror. "I decided a few minutes ago that you're a really unhappy person. I mean, I had already decided. Digby told me, you know. He told me everything. About how your mom left for no reason, and I knew about your dad."

Betrayal. I handed him a knife and he stabbed me with it.

"He said that he felt sorry for you, that he wanted to help you. I let him. I trusted him."

"Ha." I taste metal. "Me too."

"Yeah, well, you're not in a relationship with him, Lucille. He doesn't owe you anything."

Stab. Stab. Double stab. "There's nothing going on anymore," I say. "Okay?"

She's not listening to me. "We're going to school together next year. Penn State, if everything goes according to plan. And"—her voice gives a little, and then she swallows it down—"we've been talking about getting married for two years now. I mean, when we're graduated from college and everything. And then it's like you come out of nowhere.

You're all forlorn and vulnerable and you make him — you're confusing him and it's not fair. He thinks he has all these feelings, but you know what? I'm betting it has nothing to do with you at all. I think Digby would have been sucked into anyone he cared about who was in this much trouble. He gets to play savior for a minute, feel special. He just wants that good stuff you're feeding him. Makes him feel big." She fingers the gold heart at her throat. Did Digby give it to her? "And then on top of everything you had to go and pull his sister out of the river."

I can barely stand. She backs me against the door. I don't know why I can't say anything.

"I think you suck," she says. "I felt bad for you. I was happy to let him have a friend who's a girl, even a close one. You took advantage of that. You both did. You're just a sad person trying to take another person down with you, and he's such a boy that he fell for it." She's a couple inches shorter than I am, but she seems like a towering Amazon warrior brandishing a bow and arrow inches from my face. "So you look at me and tell me that what's between you is real. Tell me that Digby would have all these *feelings* for you if you were a normal person."

I struggle to find words, but I'm frozen.

"You have nothing to say to me?"

"You're right," I manage. "I'm sorry. It's done now, okay?"

Something in my stomach is ripping away, and I don't want her to see it.

She softens. "The two of you, it's a fantasy. Not real. Nothing even close to real."

This I can't let her get away with. "It felt real," I say. "It felt like the only real thing. But I am sorry, so sorry, I fell in love with your boyfriend." If I am trying to tell the truth, that is what I have.

"You hurt me. Maybe you don't care about that, maybe I don't mean anything to you, but you know, you hurt him too." She pulls her keys from her purse. "Don't do it again."

Day 4

I pick myself up the next morning and I go to school. Wren seems to be better too, so I coax her into the car with promises of shopping after. I can't stand to see her in her ratty clothes that don't fit anymore. I have to start somewhere. When you are at your weakest, when everything is a mess, cleanup has to start from the bottom. What would Eden do if we met at the rock right now? Besides tell me really smart things, she would make a list, start with reality as it is.

If I don't pull it together, my grades are going to slip, and I won't be able to stop the disaster train from driving all over me again. I slurp on a to-go cup of coffee and I assess the damage.

The facts are these:

Fred knows.

Janie knows something.

Digby knows.

Elaine knows, so her friends probably do too.

Eden knows, but she's laid out, so that's not an immediate threat.

The facts are also these:

I have lost Digby.

My best friend is in a coma.

My dad is a selfish shell.

My mom is a wandering lost person.

But . . .

I have this house.

Someone is watching over me.

I have a job.

I have a sister.

My grades are all but destroyed, but I can fix that.

I pulled Eden out of the river. I can do this. I can.

School is a land mine. Here, at the locker next to mine, the surreal Eden shrine. And after months of me never seeing her, Elaine is literally around every corner, giving me evil ice glares. I duck into the bathroom, trying to figure how I went so long like we were in some parallel universe. Now it's like she's been cloned and Multi-Elaine is out to get me.

I sit outside at lunch. Listen in class. Actually pay attention.

Get through it. Just get through this day. Worry about the other ones later.

I have other things to take care of.

First things first. My sister. After I buy her an outfit, I'm going to take her to see Dad.

They're a ways away from me, taking the walk I couldn't, Wren decked out in new glittery Melanie-ish duds. She is telling Dad everything. I know she is. I can tell from the way he hunches over her, rests his hands on her shoulder.

I read once how kids who have been beaten or abused in all sorts of horrible ways—they just want to be back home when they're taken out. They want their familiar comforts. They want to forgive. Everything in them wants that. They don't have the kind of defenses that let them see when they've been wronged. It seems warped on some level, but there's something so pure about it too. Something that gets lost in translation when you start growing up for real.

And Dad. Now we know he can lose it, because he did, so I don't think I can ever feel the same way about him again, but they love each other, at least. I can see it in how she lets him touch her, leans into him, how he perks up and smiles. It's what he needs, I guess.

"Want some coffee?" Carlos hands me a foam cup.

"Thank you," I say. "This must be a fun job."

"Something honest about it," he says. "Your pops, he's going to be all right. You'll see. When he gets out. He's solid."

"Solid as a rock."

"Yeah," Carlos says, "you need to lower your expectations some. Nobody is really a rock. That guy"—he motions to Dad with his square chin—"he spent too long pretending he was a rock. He knows not to do that anymore." His walkie-talkie buzzes twice. He checks it. "I have to go. You enjoy that coffee."

Dad still seems shifty around me, pulling on his sleeves, not quite steady in his stance, like he's holding on to Wren to keep standing.

"Will you guys be okay until I get out?" he asks. "Do I need to get you out of that house?"

"No," I say. "We'll be fine."

"I thought your mom had you. I thought it would be better if I kept out of it."

"Yeah," I say. I've put a row of dents almost all the way around the cup of coffee, and he has interrupted my pattern.

"I'm going to see if I can get some cash sent your way, okay?"

"Dad—"

"Just let me handle it." And now he does look at me. The waffle shirt under his scrubs has thumbholes in it, just like every shirt he owns.

"Give Dad hugs," I say. "We have to go. One more stop before the day is done."

His hand on my arm. "I'm sorry, Tigerlily. About Eden. But I'm proud of you. You did a good thing." I'm not expecting to feel as much as I do, for him to have just about knocked the wind out of me with his words. "Really," he says. "You're a warrior. Maybe we all lean on you a little too much, because we know you can take it. We shouldn't do that. When I'm out of here, all of that is going to change."

"It's fine," I say. "Come on, Wrenny."

Dad walks us to the door, "I'm doing everything, like you said. Talking in therapy. Even starting a job next week."

"That's good, Dad," I say. "Really."

"You know what I've been thinking about lately?"

"What?" I ask.

"The ocean. The Pacific. Surfing, smooth over waves. I was really good at that back in the day. I'd like to do that again. So think about that. Maybe when I'm out, we should go. It's a nice life out there."

"Maybe," I say. "Either way, it's probably a good thing to think about. I'm glad you're thinking about that kind of stuff."

"Yeah," he says. "Me too. I'm almost there, Tigerlily. Okay?"

Before Flowery House Manager lets us out into the night, Dad hugs Wren so her feet don't touch the ground.

"Are you mad I told him?" Wren asks as we wait for the car to warm up.

"Nah," I say. "I wouldn't have taken you there if I expected you to keep it secret." I take my gloves off and put my hand in front of the heater vent. She does the same, and our pinkies almost touch. "I've been thinking a lot lately, about secrets."

"And?" she says. She looks like a teenager.

"Secrets are bad news. Everybody has them, I think. Or they have things they don't want to share about themselves, things they aren't ready to tell. Some things stay special longer when they're private. But some other things, they get rotten when you can't say, and me asking you to keep secrets, even for a good cause . . . well, I don't think it's right for you." I turn, put my knee up against the console.

"Okay, then can I tell you something?"

"Anything," I say.

"I want Melanie to come over and play."

I surprise myself with a laugh. "Of course," I say. Instead of having friends over, she has been doing her schoolwork and entertaining herself by watching TV. Not anymore. That's done. "You can have Melanie over whenever. Tomorrow if you want. We're going to work this out. Do you believe me?"

Everything hinges on her answer. If she believes it, I will too.

"Yes," she says, "because you're you."

We stop by the hospital on the way home. I peek through the little window, and there's Janie, reading to Eden from a Kindle. Digby is not here. Perfect. I take Wren to the drink machine, buy her some hot cocoa, and ask her to stay put outside the room. Lovely Rita has her in hand when I go into Eden's room.

"Hi." I approach Janie as carefully as I can, but the Kindle still jumps.

"Some poetry," she says. "I don't know if it helps."

"I'm sure it does." I see Janie's sagging face. "You must be exhausted."

"Would you like to sit down?" She pulls on the chair next to her.

When I'm in it, I say, "I don't have very long. Wren is outside. But I'd like to talk to you about my mother."

When I get home, there is a basket of muffins on the porch.

"Thank you!" I yell into the night.

I hope somebody hears me.

Then we go inside. I bring the CD player down the stairs and plug it in, and Wren and I have a dance party, because, as Wren says, sometimes you gotta dance it out.

Day 5

The next day we wake up slow, meander around the house. I bundle us in winter gear, and we take our time. No point in rushing when late has already happened. We walk the four blocks to Wren's school on the tow path. I haven't been since the accident, and we shuffle along. Wren is too big to hold hands now, but she takes mine in hers, firmly.

"I was thinking since you don't have to work tonight maybe I'd make chicken piccata. The angel left us some capers last time, and Giada has a great recipe for it."

"Okay." I want to say so much more than that, things

about being proud and being scared, but there's been too much of that lately.

Our feet sink into new snow.

"Sometimes being late is a good thing," I say.

"Yeah." She squeezes my hand, and I know it's not only because she's happy to be with me, walking like this, it's also because this is the place where I would dip down to get to the train car, to get to the rock. I squeeze Wren's hand back, tight, and we walk the rest of the way in silence, a few lone birds crackling from the barren trees.

I don't know what's wrong with the car, but it won't start when I try to go to the hospital after school. I can get around that, I guess, but the fact that I have no phone and I don't know who I would call—it's too much. I collapse onto our porch, and Wren sits next to me. I let my head ease into her shoulder. It's frigid, but I don't have the energy to go inside.

You know how people talk about crying sometimes feeling like waves rolling over them? I've never understood that until now, but when the first wave hits me, it's like I'm holding on. I'm holding on and gritting against it. My eyes fill and I won't—won't let the tears win. But then they do, and I give in. They burst past everything, and I gasp like I'm choking on them and then I sob. Big, gulping sobs that I can't control. Wren holds on to me for real, then, both arms around me. I'm on the street and I'm losing it, and waves come as fast as they go, barely giving me time to recover from one before the next comes. This is drowning. This must be what drowning feels like. But then something that has been trapped inside me is leaving, making room, and it stops. All of it stops just when I think it never will. As quick and fierce as it came, it leaves me be. I'm empty.

The wave took something with it.

"I love you," I say to Wren. "I mean it."

"We'd better find a way to get to the hospital," she says, "if we're going to get back in time for me to make us dinner."

"I'll take you," Mrs. Albertson says from behind us.

Mrs. A wants to wait, to give us a ride home, but I assure her that we'll be fine, that Janie and John are here and we'll make it back okay, and Wren and I shuffle out of the car and onto the sidewalk, slosh through the melt, and squeak our way through the halls.

When we get to Eden's room, Digby, Janie, and John are

there, Janie and John in chairs and Digby alone at the foot of the bed. It's just a split second before they register that we're here, but it's long enough that I get to see again what a family looks like when nobody is watching.

It looks like lucky.

Janie immediately stands up. "Lucille!" she says, and she gives Wren a hug, then checks her forehead. "I wasn't sure you were going to make it here today."

"I'm sorry," I say. "My car wouldn't start."

"We got a ride from Mrs. Albertson."

Janie goes sharp for a second but softens almost right away. "I'm sorry," she says. "You could have called me."

I am trying so hard not to look at Digby or to wonder where Elaine is, and Eden is the palest I've ever seen her. She is shrinking.

"Nothing?"

"Not yet," John says. No one says anything, and he glances around. Then, as though this whole thing is too much for his sensibilities, he picks himself up out of the chair. "The belly doesn't seem to know there's a crisis at hand. I'm going to get some bad hospital grub. Anyone want anything?"

"I'll go with you," Janie says.

"You will?" John looks completely shocked.

"I will," she says, "and Wren will come too."

She's leaving Digby and me alone and not being very subtle about it. Our conversation yesterday took an odd turn. I told her more than I ever expected.

"Okay," Wren says, a little dubiously, "but I have dinner plans tonight, so I don't want to ruin my appetite."

"How about a hot chocolate?" Janie says, "and you can tell me about these plans of yours."

"Well, come on, ladies." John looks from me to Digby like he's trying to piece something together. "Maybe you can explain to me what's going on," he says to Janie on their way out.

I want to pull my skin off my body so I can crawl into it without the eyeholes and disappear into myself, never to emerge again. I want to bound across the room and hurl myself into Digby's arms like one of those cowgirl types at the end of a rom-com movie. I want sunlight and a horse or two standing by while he spins me in circles. The first option seems more plausible, but neither one possible, so I grip the metal on the bed extra tight to keep me steady. I am on a boat, rolling, cracking. I have no sea legs.

I feel him more than I see him, coming closer.

I feel him more than I see him, putting his hand next to mine on the bed.

I feel him, then I see him, fold his hand over mine, in between each of my fingers. He rests his hand just there.

"Elaine?" I say.

He shakes his head.

That's when he kisses me. Different from all the times before. Not like he's going to die if he doesn't. Not like he's stealing it. Like he's taking it. Like he's giving it.

Like he's giving in.

Eden doesn't wake up from her coma. There's no fanfare. No announcement of her spectacular recovery. She doesn't call anyone's name. She just lies there. Nothing else happens except that Digby gives Wren and me a ride home.

Digby never lets go of my hand. Not when his parents come back to the hospital room. Not when we walk down to get in the car or when he shifts gears, even. That's what happens, I guess.

Digby holds my hand.

⚡

What I find when we get home scares the living bejesus out of me. At first it looks like there are shadow creatures doing some kind of freaky rite around my car, but as the Beast shines a light on the scene I see that it's Mrs. Albertson and Andrew and Smoking Guy all standing around the open hood.

Digby lets go of me and says, "What's this?"

"I have no idea," I say.

"Angels! Angels!" Wren bounces, all the poise gone back out of her right now. "They're the angels!"

"Holy moly," Digby says. "I think she's right."

"Needs a new battery," Smoking Guy says. He's so skinny, he practically goes missing when he stands sideways.

I'm trying to figure out what's going on, and there's just no way, no way that this is the explanation. I'd sooner believe in fairies, leprechauns, gremlins. Why is that?

"I'll bring one over in the morning," Smoking Guy goes on. "Should be a ten-minute thing. No big deal."

"Say thank you," Digby whispers down to me.

"Thank you," I mumble.

Andrew looks nonplussed. "My dear Mrs. Albertson, I thought you said she wouldn't be back until later."

"Well, I didn't think so soon."

"Your lack of fairy-godmother skills is appalling," Andrew says. "If you aren't careful, I'm going to strip you of your wand."

Mrs. Albertson giggles.

Smoking Guy pulls his jacket straight and rolls his eyes, then takes the rod out of the car hood and lets it fall shut.

"I'm going to call it a night," he says.

"Karl, you come back here," Andrew says. His black cashmere coat is brushed and clean. I can see that even in the dark, even as my mind is trying to catch up to the truth.

Smoking Guy — Karl, I guess — rocks back on his heels and lets out an irritated whistle.

"So you guys are . . . what?" Digby asks, blowing into his hands. "Some kind of vigilante do-gooder co-op?"

"We saw a need," Mrs. Albertson says.

"You're good." Wren takes Mrs. Albertson's hand. "You are a amazing person."

I am in an alternate reality where people are nice and do things just because, and I can't find my feet.

"Karl is a friend of your mother's, you know," Andrew says.

"'Friend' might be overstating things. She helped me

out once, Laura did," he says. It's a raspy sort of quiet, like a voice that's not used to working. "I try not to forget."

I'm afraid to ask, but I have to. "Do you know where she is?"

"Sorry," he says.

"Or if she's coming back?" I press.

When he shakes his head, I let go of that momentary leaping hope that somehow they were all just temporarily covering for her, knowing she was on her way home.

"Would you want her if she did come back?" Karl asks me.

I don't know. I've never thought about this before. Would I? Will I want Dad? I just don't know.

"Why would you ask this girl such a question?" Mrs. Albertson barks.

I can suddenly picture the three of them in my house, in the store, fighting over what to get. The potpies had to be from Andrew. Smoking Guy mowed the lawn. Mrs. A probably cleaned the house and baked the muffins. Then I get it.

I never had any secrets. Not really.

"Why didn't you say something?" I ask. "To me. Why didn't you tell someone, report us? Why did you do all this?"

Mrs. Albertson says, "Most people in this town knew

your mom and your Aunt Jan at one time or another. Gosh, I remember when they were kids and I lived down the street in the big house. They used to come by every so often. We try to take care of our people. You girls are our people."

"What's running hard for you ran hard for them, too, back when," Smoking Guy says. "You understand?"

I do. Aunt Jan raised Mom. They didn't have parents either.

"We didn't want you to feel alone," Mrs. Albertson says, "because you're not."

"And also, being a little tricky is good fun," Andrew says.

"But now that we're here," Mrs. Albertson says, "it might be the best thing if we let someone know what's been going on. We thought your mother might be gone a little while, but now it's going on too long."

"Hang on. Hang on now," Karl says. "We talked about this."

"Karl's not a fan of the man," Andrew says, tapping his fingers on the top of the car. "Let's go inside," he says after a pause. "I have an idea."

Digby kisses my head. "I'll take Wren in the house."

Before they get to the door, Wren gives Smoking Guy Karl a freakishly long hug, which he looks like he wants to get out of like I'd want to get out of a vat of snakes.

"Okay, okay," he says, shimmying out of Wren's grasp. "That's good. Good enough." He sighs. "I told you, woman," he says to Mrs. Albertson, "some things should never be known."

It's a peculiar thing how the house changes after that. It feels fuller, somehow. Digby leaves to go back to the hospital. It's like my own empty battery recharged, and I can't sit still. I want to paint a zillion pictures and clean everything.

Chicken sizzles in the pan and pasta boils and Wren and I eat dinner, barely talking. It's good and crunchy and tender and buttery. Wren is going to be a rock-star chef someday, I swear it. She curls up on the couch and falls asleep before I can tell her to get upstairs, so I'm roaming around the house like it can answer me about what to do now. What to do until Digby comes back, until we know what's going to happen with Eden, until the rest of everything reveals itself.

⚡

One picture, even a zillion of them, won't do. Not tonight. I need more. So I paint the sky in Wren's room. I do it for her. I do it for Mom. I do it for Dad. I even do it for my dead Aunt Jan, whose breasts got sick and did her in so early and who was so much like me. Mostly, though, I do it for myself.

I'm surprised at how the brush feels in my hand. Just right, like it clicks into place, a piece of me I didn't know I was missing. Like last time. The blue covering the stains calms me.

In the morning I will be so tired, but right now I am free. I do all the cutting in, make every line perfect, and I am dancing a little myself. I take off Mom's jeans, and I am just me in my tank top and my underwear. And then I am rolling, rolling the blue blue I've Got the Blues all over everything, taking out every mark and stain and ugly that has layered our walls, and I am shaking my butt, listening to music on my headphones, even humming a little bit.

When I'm done, I take the white and I do the window frames, cover over the yellowing wood. I take my time, lost in every crease of the molding, every corner. It's bananas what paint does, how it makes everything better.

Day 7

The sun is coming up. There will be so much to do, so many more questions to ask, so many to try to answer, but right now I'm sitting in the middle of the room and I'm thinking how I made something lovely out of something so ugly. Like Andrew and Mrs. Albertson and Smoking Guy Karl did with me.

I want to understand my mother better, I think as I put all the clothes I have borrowed from her over the last months away, back into her drawers, quiet not to wake Wren. I want to know what makes a person do what she's done. I've been thinking that maybe it has something to do with the fact that her parents died when she was so young. Neither of my parents has any parents. That seems crazy to me.

Maybe Mom walked out because her sister raised her and she knew it could be done, figured I could handle it till Dad got back. Maybe she thought the two of them together were poison now and that we would be better off with just him, or maybe she's going to come back and this will all slip into a gray moment in the past.

For some people, like Janie, I think kids are what holds them to the earth, and for others, like John, it's their work. Maybe for Mom it was Dad, and without him the way she had always thought of him, she just floated away. The number 1031, the day she met Dad, was her key to everything, right? Maybe she tried to make a family with him in spite of the odds, tried to create the thing she always wished she had, and when it didn't work she fell apart.

Or maybe she didn't think at all. It's possible that she just couldn't anymore and that's as deep as it goes, I guess. I hang her skirt, the one I wore to Philly, back in her closet, then venture into my own room. It looks like somewhere I used to live. Bed made. Pictures of me and Eden. Pictures of me and my family stuck in the frame around my dresser mirror. It's cool and quiet in here.

This looks like a normal person's room, but I know what I have in me. I am a hell-breathing fire monster and I will not totter. I really did jump into a freezing river to pull Eden out. I would never walk out on Wren, and if Dad ever goes crazy again when he gets back, I will burn him up in my tiger dragon flames.

I am going to hold me to the ground because I can. And I know now how many hands I have to catch me if I fall down. Eden was wrong about some things after all. She was wrong about Digby and me. I like to think she knew that, that her soul has gotten to fly around some and when she came to visit us that night, she was telling me with her smile that she knew all the good things coming my way, that I would open my eyes and finally be able to see it all. And if it doesn't work, if Digby doesn't want to hold my hand anymore and I wind up all smashed up, I will bootstrap it until I'm whole again. Explain to me what the point of living is if you aren't willing to fight for the truths in your heart, to risk getting hurt.

You have to rage.

⚡

I lie in my bed, between my sheets, and try to let myself drift off.

But then I am missing my mom so much. I would take her back in, because I want to forgive her. I feel her smooth hand on my face, on my cheek, as my body starts to get light.

I am remembering her saying, *You have a hero's heart, Skip-to-My-Lu.*

Day 7 (still)

Almost one week since Eden, and it's been a lifetime.

The smell of breakfast wakes me up. Wren is at the stove. She's rearranged some things, put cups where plates used to be, herbs and spices within reach. Everything that was haphazard about the way Mom did things makes sense under Wren's thumb. She's so . . . efficient in there.

I'm a wreck, but I feel completely awake anyway. Maybe it's some kind of creative magic. I heard artists can stay up for days at a time when they're in a zone. It wasn't a painting on a canvas, but there was magic in it. Later I'm sure

I'll crash hard, but not now. For now I'm going to grind out this day.

I go into my bottom drawer, find my overalls, and slip them on over a black long-sleeved shirt. I brush my teeth, wash my face. As I'm drying I look at myself, and I don't hate what I see. Blue eyes. Dirty-blond hair. A puffy lower lip. Not-too-shabby eyelashes. Me. Not perfect. Not bad. Not Mom. Just me. I feel like me.

I go downstairs.

"I think I want bangs," Wren says as she flips an egg into a perfect over-easy. "Can we do that?"

"Sure," I say. "I'll ask Val where she got hers."

She pushes bread down in the toaster.

"You painted my room," she says, an elbow on the counter. "The way I wanted."

I feel myself grin.

"That's awesome." Pretty soon two gorgeous eggs and toast appear before me.

"Thank you," I say.

She takes a ketchup bottle. Writes LOVE YOU across my eggs all in red.

I don't like ketchup on my eggs and she knows this, but

today I eat them anyway and the ketchup is a sloppy kind of sweet.

"I don't want to go to Fred's anymore. It makes me tired. I can stay home alone," she tells me.

She's determined. I can see that in the way she's rinsing off the frying pan.

"I have to talk to you about something."

She turns off the water.

"Mrs. A said maybe she could watch you, maybe sleep here until my birthday or until Mom or Dad come back. If that happens."

"It will."

"Yeah. You're probably right."

I can feel Mom, out there somewhere. The waves are going to roll her back through the door. I don't expect she will be holding me up, though. I expect to catch her where she falls.

"Anyway," I go on, "Mrs. A would still mostly be at her house, but that way if anyone comes to look at the house and see how we're doing, they'll be able to see that we have someone helping. Like if you do talk to that lady at school or something. Because like we said, you don't have to keep secrets anymore." Wren only briefly stops what she's doing, then goes back to it. "She's going to be in Mom's room sometimes, okay?"

"Okay," she says.

"So I'm going to go back in my room, and you're going to go back in yours, okay?"

"Okay," she says. "Do you think she likes to bake?"

A glob of butter slides across her shirt when she goes to eat her toast.

Which is when there's a knock at the door. It could be one of about ten people at this point. Maybe it's Smoking Guy, coming to bring the battery for the car. It's not, though. It's who I hoped it would be.

"Hi there, Digby Jones," I say to his beautiful face, take his sweet hand in mine.

"Hi there, Lucille Bennett." He's wild, a wild thing standing there, like everything got loosed at once.

"What's going on?" It's barely seven thirty. I tug at him. "Do you want to come in?"

No, he tells me. He wants me to come out. Wren too. Right now.

Because she blinked.

Eden blinked.

Acknowledgments

The writing of a book (this one, anyway) is a long and winding road, one impossible to contend with in the absence of many hands, much inspiration, and the creativity of an entire city, never mind a village. To start, without my brother Chris — we aren't twins, but I wouldn't be without you, would NEVER be without you. Without my super-rebel parents, Dhyan Eagleton and Michel Meiffren; my brother, Gabriel, and sisters Renee, Celeste, and Lili; my twenty-some cousins; and my many uncles and aunties, I would probably be much better adjusted and therefore would never have written this novel. So thank you for being the brave wildlings you all are.

Joy Romero, Jessie Woodall, Laine Overley, Shandra vom Dorp, and Mindy Laks, my dead body friends, I'm honored to walk this world with all of you. Niko, Satya, Kaelin, Ryder, Ruby, Oliver, Brytin, Louis, Violet, Janie, and Mechi, I love you.

Cory, thanks for not being surprised. I am so glad I had my babies with you and so grateful for our many years together.

Eliam, my writing brother-in-arms, thank you for the perfect Philly day, for all the years of friendship that came before it, and for those that will follow. You are amazing.

Stu McKee, you have been the sweetest boy BFF for twenty years. May there be twenty more.

Thanks to Alex Eagleton, Elena Eagleton, Sarah Eagleton, Dani Kraiem, Robin Eagleton, SJ Drummey, Eric Rosse, Jill Bailey, Stephanie

Payne, Tobias Duncan, Elisa Romero, Laura Evelyn, Amanda Jane, Amber Pinnow, Charly Mabry, Prairie Rose, Jesika Brenna, Zena Hodges, Robert Sandoval, Oliver Charity, David Adjmi, Bonnie Pipkin, Tessa Roehl, Rachel Bell, Anais Rumfelt, Andrew Nowick, Cynthia Olguin, the whole vom Dorp clan, Dora McQuaid, the Robinsons, Erin Eagleton, Ted Wiard, Lisa Lastra, and Pamela Pereyra, for your general badassery. Each of you in some way made this book possible, whether by accidental inspiration, with drives across the country, kind words in difficult moments, or in leading by example with your fierce creativity and resilience. I am lucky beyond measure to know each of you, to have you in my life.

Thanks to my mother for dragging me kicking and screaming and angry as all getout into this raw, passionate, open, free-thinking, crazy, unbridled, gifted, radical, and breathtaking community at the age of fourteen. Taos, you are my heart, my heart, my heartbeat. Chef Frederick Muller of El Meze Restaurant,

273

thanks for allowing me the use of your name and likeness. You're a genius. Kitchen-style thanks also to everyone at Taos Pizza Out Back for dealing with my squeals when the book news came through, and for jumping up and down with me.

I would be nowhere at all without Vermont College of Fine Arts and its hallowed Hogwarty halls. Everyone from the administration to each of its wise and generous faculty members has given me a home and a writing family to be proud of. Special thanks to Sharon Darrow, who took me in; April Lurie, who encouraged me to dig deeper; A.M. Jenkins, who taught me to identify an emotional lie on the page and consequently in my body and consequently in my life; Martine Leavitt, who taught me that when there is nothing, you aren't a ninny, you bootstrap and build; and to Susan Fletcher, who caught the little things and who is one of the kindest women I know.

To my unofficial mentor Matt de la Peña: I will never forget reading *I Will Save You* and thinking, "I want to do THAT." And then you became my friend, which totally proves my point that magic lives. Laura Ruby, the best first reader EVER: that was a lucky playdate, and if I believed in coincidence — well, but I don't. MAGIC IFs: you're the coolest new best family of friends. Love you. YAM!

Many thanks to my Folio family, and to Emily van Beek in particular. Emily, you are not only the most wondrous agent ever, you are a stellar boss, and a dear friend. You were not afraid of leaping with me, and for that, I am yours for life. I also owe a great debt of gratitude to Molly Jaffa for her work on the foreign front. And thank you to every foreign territory that fought for me and made this novel even more of a dream come true. To Elizabeth Bewley, my fantastic editor, and everyone at HMH, thank you for taking a chance on me and for being wonderful every day since. I knew as soon as I opened your letter that you were the one.

I am infinitely, infinitely grateful to every

single person who picks up this novel, to every person who makes reading important, who finds the exploration of other worlds worthy of their time, and who shares that time with me.

My gorgeous children, Lilu and Bodhi, my reasons for breathing, thank you for your patience, your love, your hugs, and just for being. This is for you.

Finally (sigh), Chris who is not my brother Chris, I told you I didn't know how to write you a song, so I wrote this instead. Like you and Cormac McCarthy said, beauty and loss are one.

But beauty trumps.

Love.

LOOK FOR ESTELLE LAURE'S NEW BOOK

Waking from a coma, once cynical Eden sees the world in a new light and opens her heart to unfamiliar firsts, including love with Joe, a boy searching for answers to life's big questions. Lyrical, unexpected, and romantic, Estelle Laure's new novel is about interwoven lives, long goodbyes, and the imperfect beauty of young love.

ESTELLE LAURE believes in love, magic, and the power of facing hard truths. She has a BA in theatre arts and an MFA from Vermont College of Fine Arts in writing for children and young adults, and she lives in Taos, New Mexico, with her family. Her work is translated widely around the world.

Photo by Zoë Zimmerman

LEARN MORE AT ESTELLELAURE.COM AND FOLLOW ESTELLE ON TWITTER @STARLAURE.